AN AFFINITY WITH MAGIC

KATE DARBY

authorHOUSE®

AuthorHouse™ UK
1663 Liberty Drive
Bloomington, IN 47403 USA
www.authorhouse.co.uk
Phone: UK TFN: 0800 0148641 (Toll Free inside the UK)
        UK Local: 02036 956322 (+44 20 3695 6322 from outside the UK)

Published by AuthorHouse 07/26/2021

ISBN: 978-1-6655-9161-4 (sc)
ISBN: 978-1-6655-9162-1 (hc)
ISBN: 978-1-6655-9160-7 (e)

Print information available on the last page.

Any people depicted in stock imagery provided by Getty Images are models,
and such images are being used for illustrative purposes only.
Certain stock imagery © Getty Images.

This book is printed on acid-free paper.

Because of the dynamic nature of the Internet, any web addresses or links contained in
this book may have changed since publication and may no longer be valid. The views
expressed in this work are solely those of the author and do not necessarily reflect the
views of the publisher, and the publisher hereby disclaims any responsibility for them.

This book is dedicated to my sons, Ben and Mark,
who encouraged me to read fantasy to them from
a young age, and to invent stories for them.

1

Sarra's eyelids fluttered, but her eyes stayed shut against the sunlight falling on her face. She heard a boat being dragged across the shingle outside. Both things told her that she was rising later in the morning than she had intended. She swung her legs out of bed and sat up before opening her eyes. Her stomach still ached, despite the passage of time. Her sister had warned her to expect bleeding, but not this dragging feeling inside. She washed, using the water she had put aside last night and dressed using the wadding and under things her sister had given her, but ignored Aquila's dress, folded at the bottom of the basket, dressing in her customary tunic and trews.

Leaving the shade of the house she stepped into the sunny courtyard. She saw the bowls of yoghurt, dried fruits, nuts and honey on the table and felt a stab of shame. Her father must have set them out for breakfast as her sister was not yet home.

She determined to do better with the rest of the day – she was not ill and the process of growing up came to everyone! She helped herself to food, eating quickly and then clearing away. She moved first to the chickens with a basket of grain, feeding them and gathering the eggs, before stowing them in the kitchen and heading for the goat's field, jar in hand. She snagged the three-legged stool in her other hand before reaching their milking goat, Hella. Settling herself on the stool with her head resting on Hella's flank, Sarra began milking. She did not always talk to Hella, but it was soothing for them both.

"I became a woman yesterday, Hella, but as I haven't told anyone yet, I guess it's not official. It would not have felt right moving into

1

a dress with no one knowing and no one to see either. Maybe I will change when Papa gets home from fishing, or Aquila from her latest commission, if she gets back today."

Sarra paused in both the milking and talking, to wave away a fly which was bothering them, then continued.

"I'm wearing the padding and under things Aquila left for when it happened, but that was a necessity. You don't have to bother with things like that, and we can take you to visit Jerry anyway to give you a kid. It means that I could have a baby now if I wanted, but there is not anyone I like enough to marry and set up home with. With being on my own so much when Papa is fishing or on commissions and Aquila and Fern away on commissions too, I do not think that a baby would be a good idea anyway, I've enough to do here without a baby to tend, though it would be company. From what Aquila said it is more likely, now, that I develop an affinity for an element, too, if I am going to, that is."

When the usually patient goat skittered sideways, Sarra realised that, distracted as she was, she had milked her dry.

Back in the kitchen, Sarra poured half of the milk into a jug and mixed the rest with the remainder of the breakfast yoghurt, setting it aside for tomorrow. Rinsing the jar in the courtyard fountain, she then used it to take water to the seedlings on the shelves around the walls of the courtyard, before moving out to the garden.

The garden was sited behind the house and had a stream running through which her mother had created along with the garden itself. Since her mother's death in the Mage Wars, it had been tended first by Aquila and more recently by Sarra as part of their house duties. After weeding and sowing more seeds in shallow drills, Sarra watered the seed drills and then the growing crops. Returning the water jar to the kitchen, Sarra lit a cooking fire and put eggs to boil, then took a basket to the garden to gather salads and vegetables for the next two meals. By the time the eggs were cooked and cooled, and the salads washed, Arron had returned from fishing. Sarra went to greet him as he dragged his boat, 'The Swallow', up the beach.

"Hello, Papa. Were you successful?"

Arron heaved a large basket of fish out of the boat and onto the shingle. "A good basketful of whitefish for drying and eating, and a pot of squid for market tomorrow." he replied, kissing his daughter's cheek.

Sarra turned to head towards the house.

"Lunch is ready on the courtyard table, Papa. I am sorry I wasn't up to prepare your breakfast this morning, but I wasn't feeling well."

"Are you feeling better now, Sarra?" Arron's voice was full of concern.

"I just ache, Papa, but it must be to do with my bleeding, now."

"Hopefully, that will ease in time and there may be ways of dealing better with it, but you should talk to Aquila or Kiera, as they have to live with it too. We must also see Kiera about re-clothing you, it isn't fitting for you to wear trews, now."

Arron gazed tenderly down at his daughter "My little girl has turned into a woman."

Arron and Sarra ate well on salads and eggs, Arron fetching some home-made light ale to wash it down with and to toast his daughter's coming-of-age.

"We will use something better to toast the occasion when Fern comes home and brings Sten to visit."

"Will they be coming soon, then?" Sarra asked.

"Yes, they are planning to be here on your naming day. Now we can celebrate that and your coming of age together. I wanted them both here with Aquila, anyway, so that they could all talk to you about how they discovered their affinities. You may not develop an affinity for an element, but it is as well for you to be prepared."

Arron finished his ale and stretched.

"I am going to rest awhile, during the heat before I start to rack the fish, why don't you lie down for a bit too, to ease your pains, it always seemed to help your mother?"

They went to their respective rooms to rest during the heat of the afternoon. Sarra felt better for lying down but could not get to sleep straight away. She went over what her father had said, in her mind. She knew that Affines often discovered their affinities with coming of age; with working closely with other Affines; or with some sort of trauma or crisis. Her father seemed to think that this could happen to her, although most people had no magic. She had both parents and a brother and sister with an affinity, but was this a family trait, or was it random? She did not know.

Sarra didn't want to disappoint her family but had felt no attraction for any element so far and couldn't think which of the four elements was more likely to attract her. She used a lot of water in growing her plants, of course. Both her mother had been, and her sister was, a Water Affine, but she had never felt she would be able to manipulate it as they did. Her father was an Air Affine, but although he had taught her to sail when she helped him fish, she couldn't persuade the wind to do her bidding, but just use it in a conventional way, by setting the sails. Her brother was a Fire Affine, but although she often lit cooking fires, she could only light them in accepted fashion, usually using the glass Fern had given her, or sometimes a flint, and she could not make them burn excessively hot, as he did for making pots or glass. Fern's friend Sten was an Earth Affine, but although she always had her hands in the soil, couldn't detect minerals, or metals, or faults deep in the earth as he could.

Sarra didn't think she would develop an affinity for any of the four elements, but anyway, if she did, who would tend the goat and chickens and look after the garden and the bees while she was at Mage College? Who would look after the house when her father was fishing or when he, her sister or her brother were away fulfilling commissions? Who would take care of her father or take his catch to market? She had a role that was as important as any other, hadn't she? She looked after her father and their home, grew much of their food and made herself an income from selling seeds and seedlings, honey and excess garden produce at market, in addition to saving her father taking his fish to market himself. She had a role within the family, within the community, (no-one grew stronger plants than she did), and was content with her life as it was, for now.

As for her future: she had the skills to make someone a good wife one day and could live without magic! She had even used the sea like a garden, bringing live razor clams back from a fishing trip and putting them in the sea next to their sand beach, creating a new colony, near at hand, for her to harvest, and had thought of doing the same for mussels on the rocks near to the point.

Sarra must have fallen asleep at some point because she woke to find Aquila sitting beside her, on the edge of her bed.

"Ah, you are awake! I was beginning to think you would sleep until dinner time."

"No," protested Sarra "I will cook fish and vegetables for us, for dinner. I have vegetables ready, and father caught whitefish."

"I know he did, he's busy gutting most of it and hanging it on the drying rack, and I will cook dinner. It seems that you need to visit Aunt Kiera to see if she can make you some dresses, since you scorned my old one. I see you're still in trews despite becoming a woman, or so Papa tells me."

"I started bleeding this morning," confessed Sarra "but couldn't face gardening in a dress."

"I've no doubt you will get used to it. Everyone does get used to doing chores in a dress, but you will need more than one dress, anyway, and Papa has left you some coin to take to Aunt Kiera. If you leave soon you can be back by the time I've cooked dinner."

Aquila pressed some coins into Sarra's hand as she rose from the bed.

Aunt Kiera and Uncle Seth lived near the centre of the nearby town of Corvanna and Sarra walked there regularly.

"I won't be gone long." Sarra insisted. "I'll take Aunt Kiera some eggs too, it will save carrying them when I go to market tomorrow."

Sarra was used to walking into the town and usually with more than just a few eggs in her basket, so was soon approaching the first houses. She found that the brisk walk eased her aches and improved her mood. She had set out resenting the changes being forced on her by her body and by her family's expectations: gardening in a dress was stupid and would be messy and she did not want to waste Papa's money on dresses when she would far sooner wear trews anyway!

Uncle Seth and Aunt Kiera's house was near the market square, as Aunt Kiera used the front room to weave and display her lengths of linen. Sarra entered through the open door and placed the basket of eggs on the table. Her cousin Guyon was seated at the loom, receiving instruction from her mother who was standing behind her. She turned as she heard Sarra enter.

5

"Ah Sarra, Aquila came by earlier and invited us over to celebrate your name-day in a few days. She said that Fern and Sten will be back for it too. It is good that you'll all be together this year." Kiera held her sister's children in great affection and longed to mother them.

"Yes, but that isn't what brings me this afternoon, Aunt." explained Sarra. "I have need of some dresses, and Papa has sent me with some coin to buy them, if you could oblige, please."

"Of course, but your first dress has to be a present from me! I have it for you, already." said Aunt Kiera.

Then turning to Guyon, "There is a parcel under my bed, wrapped in cream linen with a blue tie around it. If you could get it for me, please?"

Guyon scuttled away and up the stairs.

"The wrapping is a night-shift, and the tie is the belt of the dress. The dress is edged with the same blue, although green might have been better for you. We'll edge the next dress with green." The last part was directed at Guyon, who had returned with the parcel.

"I can't accept something so expensive as a gift." protested Sarra. "My father sent me with coin, and I have some earnings of my own."

"No, no." insisted Kiera. "The least I can do for my poor, dead sister is to provide her daughters with the first of their dresses, it's an early coming-of-age present. We are bound to be celebrating that along with your naming day. It's a good thing that Fern intended to be here for your name-day, and I think that friend of your brother's, Sten, is very fond of you too. Perhaps he'll ask to walk out with you, now you've come of age."

"Oh, no, I'm sure he won't! Sten is just a friend, like another brother, really." said Sarra blushing.

Sarra felt most uncomfortable as to where their conversation was leading them and cut her visit short, leaving the eggs and the coins and asking for three more dresses to be made, which Kiera insisted must be accompanied by undergarments and another night shift, included in the price. Sarra said that Aquila would have dinner ready, and she must go.

"I will see you tomorrow at market, anyway. Papa has squid for me to bring and I have salad crops and sweetcorn plants."

Kiera had hoped that Sarra would change into the dress but had to be content with her promise to wear it to market the following day and watched her leave with the parcel tucked into her basket.

Despite her saying she needed to hurry, Sarra found the time to exchange pleasantries with several people on her journey home.

"Hello, Sarra, I caught sight of Aquila heading home, is she staying for a while this time?" Niome was the same age as Aquila and missed her company when she was away fulfilling commissions.

"I don't know, Niome, I haven't really had time to talk to her yet, but she'll be here until my name-day in a few days' time, at least."

Sarra moved her basket to her other arm as Niome seemed to be taking great interest in her parcel, and there were things that she was not yet ready to share, then nodded and moved on. "I'll tell her you asked."

"Good afternoon, Sarra, will you be at the market in the morning?"

"I will, Brewer Fester. Papa has some fresh squid for me to bring to market to sell." replied Sarra. "And I have an excess of salad leaves in the garden, which I am hoping to bring too."

"Well, I have none left in my garden, so save some for me." Brewer Fester replied jovially. "Will you have squash plants for sale?"

"I will have sweetcorn plants but was going to leave the squash plants to grow for another few days. I could put a couple into the basket for you if you would like?" Sarra knew that he liked to be planting ahead of his neighbours.

"I would appreciate that, Sarra."

"You haven't any work for a school-friend, have you Sarra?" butted in a slightly drunken Wessus. "I can dig and water and carry stuff to market for you."

"Don't do it, Sarra, he is useless, I've tried giving him work and he won't even be awake at that time in the morning. Carry things to market, indeed!" advised Fester.

"Thank you for offering, Wessus, but I have only enough work for me at the moment, and none to spare."

Their conversation was interrupted, yet again, by another passer-by: "There are some of our class-mates not worth speaking to, Sarra, haven't you learned yet, that Wessus is one of them?" Janus spoke in a condescending tone from the back of his donkey.

"There are a lot of people who I went to school with that I choose not to socialise with, Janus, and many that I do, but the choice is still mine!" Sarra's tone was sharp and cool.

You tell him, Sarra." Wessus was now using Janus' donkey as support.

"Goodbye, Janus, Wessus. I will see you tomorrow, Brewer Fester." Sarra took her leave, with a smile and a wave for Brewer Fester.

The walk home was quick as Sarra was now free of aches and pains and was invigorated by her trip.

The smell of grilled whitefish met Sarra as she rounded the corner of the house and entered the courtyard. Her sister stood, turning the fish on the rack over the flames and her father sat at the table helping himself to vegetables from the bowls on the table.

"Just in time, Sarra." Arron placed vegetables on the platter set for her and motioned for her to sit beside him. "Have you ordered some dresses from Kiera? What is in the basket, she can't have made one in the short time you've been gone."

"Aunt Kiera had it ready for me under her bed. It's a present for my coming of age, a dress and matching belt and a nightshift."

Aquila slipped a cooked whitefish onto Sarra's platter beside the vegetables. "Yes, I remember that she did the same for me when I came of age. In fact, I think it was the dress I left for you to use, it was my favourite for many years."

"I didn't scorn the dress, Aquila, I just didn't want to trail it in the mud when I worked in the garden." Sarra was contrite.

"That is what the belt's for, darling. Wear it shorter while you work. But not too short, you aren't a child anymore." Aquila advised.

Arron placed an arm around her shoulder. "Aquila and I were talking while you were out. This is our home, yours, mine, Aquila's and Fern's, and Sten seems to have adopted it too – the guest room seems to have become his. I am usually out fishing and the three of them are often away on commissions, and me sometimes too. It seems to have fallen to you to run the home, and if that continues, we need to provide you with an allowance."

"But, Papa, I sell plants and produce at market…" Sarra interrupted, and was re-interrupted in return:

"That is what you do with your own time, to put coin in your pocket, but you have a full-time commission keeping house for us while we take commissions for coin, or I fish for profit as well as food. Anyone else taking my fish to market would take a share my takings or would charge me a fee. We can talk more when Fern and Sten are here, and could re-evaluate as or when things change again, if Aquila or Fern leaves to set up their own households. But we must talk of these things."

Aquila had paused and looked up, surprised at the idea being muted, of her leaving home. "For now, let's eat, while it is all still hot."

After a companionable meal, and when the sun reached the horizon, Arron rose and picked up a lantern. "It's a market day tomorrow and at the moment I've only squid to sell. I'd better head out into the lagoon with a light to attract some coin-earning fish – I've a celebration to pay for and dresses to buy!" He grinned to show he was joking, then dropped a kiss on top of each girl's head and headed down the beach.

After they had heard The Swallow being dragged into the water Aquila rose from her seat. "I'll lay out breakfast in the morning, if you'll tend the chickens and the goats, then I can get the fish ready for market while you get your produce and plants ready to go."

Having doled out the tasks for morning, Aquila headed for bed. "Goodnight Sister, I have missed you."

"I have missed you, too." Sarra told the retreating back.

Sarra picked up a shallow bowl from next to the courtyard fountain, dipped it to fill and headed for her room too.

Sarra woke in the dark to hear her father drag The Swallow onto the shingle, then turned over and went back to sleep.

She woke bright and early, 'how different from yesterday', she thought as she washed and dressed in her new clothes. She combed and plaited her hair and stepped out into the sunlight.

The breakfast was laid out on the table, where Aquila sat eating.

"Good morning sister." Sarra said in greeting.

"Good morning sister. It is good to be home."

"It is good to have you home. Will you be going off for a new commission soon?"

"No, I have nothing scheduled, presently. I will be here for at least a tenday or so, so I will be able to help with markets and the house chores, and it will be good to see Fern and Sten too."

"Niome asked after you, yesterday." Sarra suddenly recalled.

"Yes, it will be good to see her too, and she will know all the local news. And be in a hurry to impart it." Aquila smiled with that thought.

Having eaten, Sarra shortened her dress using the belt, donned an apron and headed out to feed the chickens and milk the goat, but not before receiving a kiss on the cheek from her father as he came out for breakfast. By the time Sarra had a basket full of salad leaves and greens for market, and many of her sweetcorn plants, not forgetting two squash plants for Brewer Fester, in a second basket, Aquila had sorted her father's catch into two baskets and was ready to leave.

As they walked to the town the two sisters chatted to each other as though they had not been apart, though Aquila did complain about the vagaries of her last commission and Sarra caught her up with some of the gossip from town. The market sellers were settling their wares on the ground as they arrived, so the sisters did the same. Sarra sat on a mat next to her crops and plants.

Aquila placed the fish baskets next to the mat.

"Can you sell father's fish? He gave me other errands to run while we are in town,"

"Of course. I normally sell both, and then must run his errands. At least you running the errands will save me time." Sarra replied.

Sarra had already sold most of her sweetcorn plants when her Aunt Kiera arrived.

"Are those all you have left, Sarra? I was going to have some from you."

Sarra smiled up at her aunt. "There are more at home, I'll set them aside and bring them for you tomorrow, when there's less to carry, as there's no market."

"It's time that father of yours invested in a donkey, and I shall tell him when I see him – building a house convenient to where he works and making my sister and her children walk into town carrying heavy loads!" said Kiera crossly.

"But Mother loved it by the beach too, and we are all used to walking. Aquila, Fern and even Father have to walk much further for their commissions."

"I can bring the plants back from your name day meal, and bring your other dresses and underthings then too, there's only two days to go. Just take this one to have another new one for on the day." Kiera passed over a parcel wrapped the same as the last, but with green ties. "Fern and Sten are due tomorrow, aren't they? I should think you will be glad to see them; it's been a long time since Fern's been home.""

"Yes, they had a large commission helping to set up a new iron working in the Hardare Mountains, they'll have been gone for nine tenights."

"Good morning, lovely ladies. That is a very nice dress, Sarra, one of your aunt's creations, I have no doubt. I see you have brought my plants." Brewer Fester beamed at the two of them.

"Thank you, Brewer Fester." Sarra blushed at the mention of her dress, as it marked her passage into adulthood. "Just two coppers each, for the plants, if you please, I won't charge you for the growing cups, because I know you'll let me have them back."

The hardened clay growing cups had been an invention of her brother's and he kept her supplied with them. They enabled her to keep the seedlings' roots intact and safely transport them. She had had many ruined seedlings when she had to dig them up out of the ground and bring them to market unprotected.

"You might not grow me any more seedlings if I didn't!" Fester laughed heartily.

Their good humour was dispelled by the arrival of Janus again, this time on foot.

"Good morning, Mistress Sarra. I see you are selling sweetcorn plants; I have three fields planted up with them." Sarra felt most uncomfortable at being referred to as 'Mistress'. Although it was now technically correct, it drew attention to her altered status.

"Indeed, Farmer Janus? It is nice to know we have one thing

in common!" Sarra's tone was cold, using his title of 'Farmer' quite deliberately. Sarra turned to chat to her aunt, and when she turned back, Janus had left.

By the time Aquila returned to the market Sarra had been sold out for some time.

"I'm sorry, father gave me a big list of people to see."

"It wasn't a problem; it gave me time to sit and chat."

They gathered up the empty baskets and made their way home. Although the journey home was relieved by the girls exchanging tip-bits of gossip they had learned in town, it had been a tiring day and they were pleased to be arriving home. They were even more pleased to hear conversation and laughter before they rounded the corner of the house and reached the courtyard.

Sarra dropped her baskets and threw herself into her brother's arms. "You're early! It is so good to have you home."

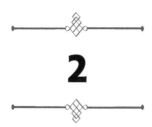

2

Fern put one arm around her to hold her close and used the other to steady himself against the stone table. "If we'd realised we would get such a welcome, we'd have worked twice as hard and got here sooner."

Sarra moved back slightly to take both young men into her sight. The two were very alike in form and stature, tall and well-muscled, but Fern was auburn haired and green eyed, like herself, and Sten had dark curly hair and dark brown eyes.

"If you hadn't been gone so long, I might not have missed you so much." Sarra laughed.

"Dinner is almost ready." announced Sten, and then to Sarra "I took the liberty of raiding your vegetable garden."

"You are most welcome, as long as they're still edible!" Replied Sarra.

"Who do you think feeds us when we're away on commissions?" asked Fern. "You know my skills in the kitchen – particularly a camp kitchen!"

Sten moved a large iron pot from the fire onto a trivet on the table and began ladling fish stew into bowls. "For me, it was a case of '*learn to cook, or starve*' – Well one of us had to when Mama died, and Papa didn't seem inclined."

They all sat and ate in silence for a while, stopping only to refill their bowls.

Arron got up to fetch the girls' beakers, there were already their three and a jar of ale on the table.

"We have been talking." he announced as he sat down again.

"Without us?" asked Aquila.

"Well, the three of us talked a bit, yesterday." said Arron, then continued: "If Sarra didn't grow our food, we'd all be forced to buy it at market, we none of us have time to grow it."

"The same applies to your fish." Sarra countered.

"Nonsense, you gather shellfish, as well." Arron quickly moved on: "Anyway, I'm your father, I'm supposed to provide for you! We aren't often available to help with house chores, but we are earning coin from commissions, and need to provide you with earnings too."

"You're not my father and have no obligations to feed me." Sten interrupted. "I am the one who is obligated."

"We have already discussed that." Arron said, dismissing the subject, then turned to the girls again.

"We are going to be putting Sten's living arrangements on a more permanent footing and build on another room, so that we still have a guest room. I first built this house for Yanna and I to live in when we married. Then it was just two rooms facing the beach, a bedroom and a living room/kitchen with storeroom off. Yanna created the garden behind it. When you came along," Arron said, nodding to Aquila. "Then I built on two more rooms, one for you and a guest room, making an 'L' shape, and paved a courtyard for outdoor eating and living. Later, when you two joined the three of us," This time nodding at Fern and Sarra. "I built on the other side, two more rooms, expanded the courtyard and extended the roof to make a veranda for moving between rooms when it rains. Apart from your mother causing the water to rise for a fountain, for fresh water to the house, it hasn't been altered since."

Arron paused to take a drink, then continued "Sten has made his home with us, and since his father is dead, he has no other home. He is willing to help with labour, so we are going to build him a room."

"I can provide coin for materials too." Sten insisted.

"You and I have already debated that." said Arron firmly. "And since you are now an acknowledged part of this family, there are other things to discuss."

Arron took time out to fetch another jug of ale from the store and to refill the water jar, before sitting again, this time to face Sarra. "You are no longer a child, learning at school or learning how to run a home, you may have plans we don't know about, to go off and marry, or to apprentice yourself as a forager, or farmer, or brewer, or something else, you have skills enough for all of those. But if we assume you are going to stay, at least for a while and look after our home, we must provide for you, from the coin we earn. It is also long past the time we had a donkey and cart for transport, it will make everyone's' lives easier and we will all contribute. You will use it more than most, but it will benefit us all. You can use it to take your produce and my catch to market, and when Aquila, Fern, Sten or I have a commission that we need to travel to, where we need to stay, you could transport us, or at least take us as far as the King's Highway and then bring the cart home. While we are building on a room for Sten, we will build on a covered cart store."

"We must also prepare you, as well as we are able, for the possibility of you developing an Affinity for an Element. We cover the four Elements between us, and can each give you a better understanding of how we developed our Affinities."

Arron stopped briefly, to refill all the beakers with ale, then he continued:

"I will begin, by talking about my affinity, though you may have heard much of this before. My Affinity grew slowly, or perhaps it was there some time and I was just slow to recognise it. As you know my father was a fisherman. He was born into a boatbuilding family who work at the northern end of the lagoon, where the Rio Roja flows into the lagoon and the wooded slopes of the Sierra Cappallla provide good timber. His three elder brothers worked boatbuilding with his father too, so when trade declined, he apprenticed himself to a fisherman, despite being a married man and with me as a child on the way by then – they had to eat, and he owned a boat that he could use. When he began to work alone, he took me out with him and taught me to sail and to fish. One day we were fishing past the reef in the Great Sea, when we were pushed far out by a squall. Coming home tacking hard against the wind, I said to him *'wouldn't it be easier to get the wind to blow where we want to go?'* and he laughed and said: *'If you can do that, you go ahead, and do it, but until then, just do what I'm telling you, with the sails.'.* I did it his way, but over time I realised that I could 'persuade' the wind to help me much of the time. I thought of it as nudging the wind with my mind, though I couldn't do it in a storm. Then later, of course, I went to Mage College and was trained to use my full potential. That's the thing about Mages, they somehow link their powers with Affines and enhance them, and through Mage College training the enhancements stay. That's why it's necessary to go to Mage College."

Aquila took up the tale next:

"The awaking of my Affinity to water was quite different and more sudden. It came from a shared experience with Mother. She was expecting you, and Papa was working hard on extending the house. Fern was still small but had moved from their bedroom into the guest room, so Papa was building the second wing of two rooms, to keep all the views of the sea, and shelter the courtyard more. That was between fishing trips; commissions as an Air Affine; and helping to look after Fern and me. Mama had given up all but local commissions as a Water Affine but was expanding the garden to grow more and sell some crops. She had been 'pulling' water from a stream near the back of the garden to water the plants, but there had not been much rain and that was getting more and more difficult. She had sown lots of seeds that day and needed to water them to start new life in them, but she was exhausted. She sat on a large stone near the top of the garden and tried and tried to pull the water nearer but there just was not enough and it seeped down into the earth as she pulled it close. She told me she could sense a larger supply but that it was further away, and she was going to try for that. I could see that she was concentrating hard and straining to pull the water, then she started to keel over sideways. I rushed to her and put my arms round her to support her and hold her upright, and I suddenly felt as though my energy was flowing into her and I could sense the water too and help her pull at it. We pulled harder and harder and I felt that it was coming up towards us, but we were both getting weaker and the world seemed to be getting darker and I think we both fainted, When I woke up I was lying on the ground with my arms still round Mama, there was cold water swirling around us and then running through the garden sweeping the soil and seeds away. Then mama wakened too and drank straight from the spring that had emerged under the rock we were sitting on. She had to replace and replant all the seeds, and re-plan the garden around the stream, but we were never short of water again, and from that time onward I could help her to move water and my Affinity increased with time, then was enhanced by my learning with the Mages at Mage College."

Aquila finished talking and turned her gaze from Sarra to Fern.

"That's quite a lot for Sarra to take in in one go," began Fern. "Perhaps, as it is getting late, Sten and I should wait until morning to relate our stories, when we'll all feel fresh?"

Sarra was about to object, but when she opened her mouth to speak, a great yawn was all that came out.

Arron laughed. "I think that answers that question, - even if Sarra was about to say 'no'!"

"You four get off to bed and I'll clear these things away and see you tomorrow."

Sarra was first up in the morning and eager to hear more of their experiences, so had laid breakfast out in the courtyard and was eating hers when the others emerged from their rooms.

Arron had his mind, though, on other things: "I need to go and make some arrangements for tomorrow, and have a couple of errands to run, so I'll be gone all of the morning, and perhaps longer. Have lunch without me, If I don't get back. I can always get something for myself."

Aquila also excused herself, claiming a prearranged visit with Niome.

Sarra's disappointment was so obvious that Fern reached across the table and squeezed her hand. "Don't worry, Little Sister, we aren't deserting you!"

Sarra brightened considerably and set about finishing her breakfast. Arron and Aquila both left the table, going to their rooms before emerging to walk together towards the town.

Sarra cleared the breakfast pots and excess food and brought jars of fresh fruit juice and water to the table with clean beakers. She found that Fern and Sten were discussing the acquisition of reef rock, limestone and state, and the process of slaking lime to make mortar, so she left them talking, to go and tend to the chickens and the goat. After dealing with those chores, Sarra stood gazing over the garden, assessing progress, and making a mental note of jobs to be done but deciding to leave the garden for that day. She heard a noise behind her and turned to find Janus standing next to her.

"A dress suits you, Sarra." He did not realise what a bad opening this was, but, getting no response, changed tactics anyway.

"Is your father at home? I was hoping to talk to him about a commission to build a windmill. I have done very well growing wheat, and bread is becoming popular. Those of us that inherited land and a business from our forefathers have a duty to keep it safe and pass it on, improved, to our children."

'Pompous ass!' thought Sarra.

But she was kinder and more diplomatic "I'm afraid he has gone into town, but I will tell him that you called."

"I would also like his permission to walk out with you." announced Janus.

'What about my permission?' Sarra thought. She was incensed but she said nothing.

"Wind is very uncertain; you might be better off to have my sister raise a spring and consider a water wheel." Sarra avoided anything personal.

"I don't normally employ women for important tasks, even women Affines." Janus announced, then just stood watching Sarra.

"I'm sorry, I will pass on your messages, but have chores to complete." Sarra made her excuses and headed around the house, and out of sight, before saying something that she would probably regret.

Fern and Sten were still talking about the building work when Sarra returned, so she brought her basket weaving to the table to keep her hands occupied. Eventually the two young men had exhausted the conversation and decided to wait for Arron to acquire the necessary materials. That could even be one of the errands he had gone to do, in which case their discussion would be wasted.

Sarra hoped that they would have time for her, now, and set her basket-making aside.

Fern took Sarra's hand began: "We do understand your curiosity,

Sarra, but there isn't really any urgency in the telling, we aren't expecting you to need all our information overnight! We will only be celebrating your sixteenth name-day and your coming-of-age tomorrow. Father obviously sees that, and the changing dynamics of the family group as his main priorities today, perhaps things will change after that, later-on."

"I can see that." Sarra acknowledged. "But it is only another name-day, and the building work he outlined will take a great many tenights." She let out a deep breath that she did not even know she had been holding.

"I may never need the information you are going to give me, I may not develop an Affinity at all, but, as you say, the dynamics within the family are changing, as is my place in it, and the better I understand the way you all work, the better I can help support you all, if that is to be my role and my destiny."

Sten took Sarra's other hand. "We none of us know our destiny, Sarra, and I think your father made it clear, yesterday, that you have lots of choices as to the role in life you want to make. You are an exceptionally talented girl...no, woman...and must decide where you want your life to take you, and what you want to do. We are the ones with limited choices. When an element chooses you, it defines who you are and makes some of your choices for you. Fern or I could not choose to be brewers, though we can both brew ale and could learn to make wine. We will always be Affines. Magic opens up one world to you, Sarra, but it closes off many more." He squeezed her hand. "It is that that your father wants you to be prepared for!"

He took a deep breath and continued: "Your father is one of the few Affines I know, who also has another job. He was a fisherman first, of course, and he does use air as part of his job, but most Air Affines would have given up fishing. There are enough commissions to be had, and few enough Affines. Your mother, too, was a gardener and food producer, as well as a mother and taking commissions as a Water Affine. It is unusual to combine anything besides motherhood with being an Affine, you normally earn coin from commissions and pay someone else to look after your needs and many Affines pay someone to take care of their children too."

"Much of that is irrelevant, though. You want to know about Fern and me becoming Affines, don't you?"

At Sarra's nod, Sten continued. "Well, I'll give you my story first."

"I grew up in the Hardare Mountains, in a small mining town close to where we were working recently. My parents both worked in a coal mine. My father was a picker and hewed coal at the front of the seam, my mother was part of a team of women who hammered it into smaller lumps and loaded it into waggons, to be towed out of the mine by oxen.

It was hard work which left people with breathing problems and a short life. I worked as hard as I could at school, hoping to be good enough to work for one of the traders in coal, iron or stone, the only good things to come out of the Hardare's."

"Apart from Sten, of course!" Fern interrupted.

"Apart from me." Sten agreed, with a grin, then continued: "I was in my last few tenights of schooling and the mine Manager had shown interest in my skills with figures. He had talked to my father about employing me to work for him, scribing tallies in his record books. I was at school and my parents were working as usual when it happened. There was an explosion that we all felt through the rock under our feet and a great cloud of dust poured out of the entrance of the mine. We all knew what had caused it, it was a known hazard of mining, bad air makes an explosion from the candles or lanterns the workers are using. Everyone reacted exactly as we were trained to and went straight to their emergency teams, digging out the fall from the entrance, working inwards, even the children get set to work. We piled the rock debris into small carts and moved it out of the way, the younger children carried messages, or brought water. The teams worked all morning and by the time they had switched teams to rest and eat, they had got to the women's carts which had been crushed in the fall and were bringing out bodies. My mother was among them. There was not time to grieve then, we worked, ate, rested, then went to work again. After the fourth change, we still had not reached the end of the fall, we had been working from mid-morning until almost dark. The Gaffers who had been off above ground started to tell the Manager that the fall might go all the way to the picking edge and there may be no survivors to reach, but I could feel it when I touched the rock, I **knew** there was a clear airspace behind the fall. The Gaffers said it was what I wanted to believe, that I had lost my mother and could not face the idea that I had lost my father too. I told them that that was true, but that I wasn't imagining there was a space, I could **feel** it through the rock."

Sten paused to take a long drink of ale. Sarra could see the strain of the grief in his face as he re-lived the experience.

"It's not something I talk about often and it is hard to explain – I hope you understand what I am trying to say. Anyway, the Gaffers wanted to abandon the mine and leave it as a grave and start a new mine from a different drift, but the Manager told them to keep digging. He took me on one side and asked me how I knew there was a void behind the fall. He was calm and sympathetic, and I trusted him, so I tried to explain it to him as I had not been able to tell the others. I told him that I could feel the air behind the rock fall, that I could taste the bad air above the fall, but the air behind did not taste of that. He asked me if I meant that I could smell it, but I said *'No, I can taste it in my mind.'*. He said that he believed me, and he trusted my judgement. It was full dark, and the moon had risen when they broke through. The men behind the fall could hear them digging the fall out and had dug towards them. They had done that in total darkness, because of the bad air, and they could not risk sparking a light. After the rescue there had been a time of mourning and re-adjustment, for many families and the whole town."

"I never did go back to school, it didn't re-open until after my nameday. So, although the mine Manager had been around all the bereaved families initially, it was a surprise when he called again. He told my father that he had come to talk about me. Father thought he was going to say that I was going to be taken-on for the tallying, but the Manager said he had talked to the Mine Owner about me, who had sent for a Mage to test me. The Mage would probably be arriving in the morning. I left with the Mage four days later, with clothing paid for by the grateful Mine Owner and the blessings of the rescued men. I never saw my father again; he was killed in another fall a few moons later." Sten sat back and took another swallow of ale. "It was at Mage

College that I ran into your brother, and I think it's time that he took over talking."

Fern began: "It was just after finishing my schooling that I discovered my Affinity for Fire. There were a group of us boys of the same age all trying to decide our future: whether to train in our fathers' crafts, apprentice to another craft, or just find labouring commissions until we decided what to do with our lives. Two days after the completion our schooling we arranged a picnic and camp on the beach just up the coast, south of Corvanna. We sailed up using Swallow and one other boat, we took ale and bread and two of us went fishing while the others gathered wood for a fire for cooking. When we returned with the catch, they had a good blaze going and had started on the ale. Poul and I gutted the fish and skewered it on to twigs to roast, while they brought us ale and kept drinking themselves. Just as I brought a load of skewered fish over towards the fire, someone stood up and lurched towards me, knocking me off my feet and into the fire."

Sarra gasped and gripped Fern's hand tightly.

"I was alright! That was the shock, the fire had been burning quite fiercely, but the moment I fell into the fire, it went out. I did not quash it by rolling on it, it just went out completely. No-one was too far gone with ale, but there was no fire to cook the fish on, and it extinguished the mood as well as the fire, so we packed up, loaded the boats and sailed home. Papa was incredibly surprised when we returned so early and thought there must have been an accident, but the others filled him in with the detail and he suggested that they just went home to bed. In the morning Mama and Papa had me trying to invigorate and quash the cooking fire which seemed quite easy and also had me trying to light one without flint and iron, or a lens, which I could not do, but Papa went off to talk to the Mages about me and I found myself going to Mage College, where I met Sten, of course. We were both from relatively poorer backgrounds and Fire Affines and Earth Affines often worked together, and we just got on like brothers, if fact some people assumed that we were brothers or cousins."

"You have to remember that it was before the Mage Wars." Sten pointed out. "There were a lot of Mages about, training Affines and new Mages. We spent time learning botany and zoology, first, then philosophy and alchemy, before moving on to magic. When it came to magic, we usually worked in groups of up to ten with each Mage, Affines with affinity for the same elements, training to do a particular thing or using different affinities together to accomplish a task."

Sarra did not really understand that. "Like what?" she asked.

"I sometimes work with a Water Affine," explained Sten. "If the water they are trying to reach is a long way underground, I might be able to open up faults in impervious rock to allow it to rise through the faults to the surface to form a spring. If I am working with a Fire Affine who is helping to heat iron ore, I can 'persuade' the iron ore to accept heat more easily and for the iron to run from the rocks with less heat. Working on a task alongside a Mage magnifies your Affinity and helps develop it but working with a group of Affines with the same affinity helps you to hone your affinity more and makes you stronger and more resilient. That has been particularly important since the decline in the number of Mages available, Affines are having to train at Mage College to cover the work that Mages did with Elementals in the past, and there is little time for the other learning that we were given."

Fern looked profoundly serious at this reminder and added: "The whole emphasis of training has changed now, Affines tend to be strengthened and encouraged to work on tasks they can complete in groups or alone, now. In the past, they would have been encouraged to have a wider education, then join a Mage in a Mage Tower where the Mage would commission for work involving all four elements, and each Mage would have four or eight Affines working with them, enhancing their powers and making them into Elementals. Sten and I spent our first few years looking for someone who enhanced our powers but did not have an Affinity for any one element, who might be a potential Mage so we could join their Tower community and become Elementals, but, of course, it never happened. Now there are few Mage Towers left."

Arron had returned and re-joined them at the table while Sten was speaking. "There used to be Mage Towers in most large towns." he echoed. "Torroja, the town in the northern part of the lagoon was named after its Red Tower, in the ancient Mage tongue, though the tower was destroyed in a dispute long before the Mage Wars. There was even a Tower on the Isla Grossa, the largest island in the lagoon, though that was destroyed during the Mage Wars."

Sten looked at Arron with interest. "Can you visit that island and tower? I'd be interested to see it."

"It was always discouraged in the past, as people thought that the Mage and Elementals that had lived there would know if it were disturbed, if they were still alive, and the horrors of the Mage War were fresh enough to frighten people away. It is probably safe to visit, but you would have to plan an expedition there, because you do not know what you might find, and it would take most of a day to sail there and back, anyway. Perhaps, if you are keen to look, we could think about it when we have finished celebrating Sarra's nameday."

"But before we start on the building work!" Fern added quickly.

"Alright, before we start the building work." agreed Arron.

Realising how much time had passed while they had been talking, Sarra left her father, brother and Sten to bring out and set some lunch on the table.

During their meal Aquila returned from the town and sat down to eat with them. "I have invited Niome, to the celebrations tomorrow, I hope that is all right with you?" Aquila's gaze took in her father and sister.

Sarra merely nodded as her mouth was full.

"Of course. The more, the merrier!" replied Arron.

"And since you don't see so much of your school friends, these days, I asked Chania and Gemma, too" Aquila continued.

"It will be good to see them again." Sarra agreed.

Speaking of school, Sarra recalled Janus' visit earlier.

"Farmer Janus called earlier, Papa, he wanted to talk to you about a possible commission to build a windmill. He also said he wanted your permission to walk out with me, and if you give it, I'll never talk to you again!" The last part came out in a rush.

Arron slipped his arm round his daughter's waist and drew her onto his lap. "I would never give anyone my permission to walk out with either of my daughters without their expressed wishes agreeing with that. I value them both too highly." Sarra hugged her father and rose to hug Aquila too.

"I'll give you a hand in the garden, after lunch." Aquila told Sarra. "We can pick salads and vegetables for tomorrow as well as tonight's meal. Tomorrow will be busy enough without that, and we can't avoid chicken and goat chores."

Arron took this as a cue to organise the two young men to help him dig a fire pit that afternoon and then for them to set up a temporary extra cooking fire to cope with the food for the next day, whilst he would then go fishing.

When they came together that evening for their meal, their appetites were large, but conversation was sparse as they all were all weary. They headed to bed before it was even full dark.

3

The girls rose late but were still up before the men. They washed and dressed but saved their finery for later. They were laying out the breakfast when they heard the rare sound of a donkey and cart in the lane behind the house. A few moments later Janus appeared around the corner swinging two plucked geese by their necks and was followed by a thin, poorly clothed youth carrying a pig's carcass draped over his shoulders.

"I hope this order is correct and I haven't come so far because of a prank!" Janus addressed Sarra and his tone was sharp and slightly belligerent.

Sarra was somewhat shocked and surprised. "A prank?"

"I know that you tend to eat fish that your father has caught and vegetables that you grow yourselves, rather than meat or vegetables bought from farmers or market. Janus continued in an aggrieved tone. "However, I have an order here, for a whole roasting pig and two fat geese."

"And has the order been paid for?" asked Sarra with forced sweetness, knowing that it must have been.

"It has!"

"Well, hardly a prank, then!" Sarra practically spat.

Sten had appeared behind Sarra, and stepped forward to take the pig, swinging it over one shoulder.

"Do you need these three moving, Sarra? They are no weight at all compared with stone." he said, relieving Janus of the fowl. "Thank you, tradesman. You can be on your way now!"

Janus flushed deeply with embarrassment and anger.

Sten moved towards the kitchen area with the meat, Sarra following.

This left Janus standing alone and feeling a little foolish. "I was hoping...."

Sarra turned back to Janus but made no move to approach him.

"We are all very busy today, preparing for a family celebration," Sarra explained. "I'm afraid Papa has no time to talk of windmills today."

Janus had been hoping for an invitation, rather than a chat about a commission, but was forced to turn away, disappointed.

Fern and Sten spitted the pig on a long iron spike and placed it over the fire pit. Fern then lit the fire that they had laid ready the day before. Sarra and Aquila lit the small cooking fire to cook eggs for lunch and began to stuff the geese with herbs and wrap them in seaweed to roast in the hot coals later. They prepared huge quantities of salad leaves for lunch and for the celebration dinner later.

Aquila was putting food onto the table and calling the others to lunch when Brewer Fester walked around the corner of the building and called out to Arron:

"I've got your delivery, I hope you've got some strong arms for lifting and carrying."

"I have, indeed. Fern and Sten will help you, I am sure. They will if they want to sample your wares, anyway!" Arron replied with a laugh.

"Brewer Fester, we were about to sit down to a little lunch." said Sarra. "Would you care to join us? It's just eggs, potatoes and salads?"

"Only if you let me contribute." replied Brewer Fester. "I brought something new for you to try, so now would be as god a time as any other! I'll just fetch them."

Brewer Fester went back to his cart and reappeared moments later carrying a basket. "As you know my wife, Hetta has been using my yeast and ground down wheat to make that new bread. She bakes big pieces of it that you can cut or tear apart and eat instead of potatoes, and it is spongy and soaks up liquid so it's good with a stew. Well, she has been trying different things with it, and she has made these little round ones you can cut in half or make a slit in, and stuff with meat or salads or cheese or eggs and eat while you're travelling. She was always on at me for being too busy to stop and eat, but now she does not have to worry, because she puts these in a basket to take with me. They make great travelling food."

Brewer Fester put his basket on the table with the other food. "They are calling the people who make this bread 'bakers'. Hetta's talking about setting up a shop next to the brewery and training someone else up to work with her too and calling herself 'Baker Hetta'! Life is full of surprises, isn't it?"

Aquila took one of the new creations from the basket and opened it to peer inside. Seeing the soft goat's cheese inside, she added spicy leaves, closed it up and took a large bite.

"What do you think?" asked Brewer Fester.

"It's wonderful." Said Aquila as soon as her mouth was free to talk. "It would be great as travelling food. What does she call it?"

"Well, she takes a small piece of dough and rolls it between her hands then flattens it, to shape before baking it, so she calls it a 'roll', when she calls it anything." explained Brewer Fester.

"It would be really good for putting in cuts off the roasted pig." said Aquila. "I wonder if she'd have time to make us some more before tonight?"

"I'll get home and ask her as soon as we've unloaded the ale and the wine. There should be plenty of time, as I know she was baking when I left, so the oven should be heated, and she can keep the fire going, I always have plenty of yeast left and I'll give her a hand if she needs it."

"Then you should both return to celebrate Sarra's nameday with us," said Arron. "With or without her 'rolls'."

They all sat down to eat the meal together, though the family and Sten were aware of all the jobs yet to be done.

When they had all eaten Arron, Fern and Sten followed Brewer Fester round the side of the house, back to the cart and returned carrying five jars of wine and rolling a large barrel of ale. Brewer Fester was carrying a barrel stand.

"When we have set up the barrel, leave it to settle and don't touch it until I return. When I come back, I'll tap it and test it. It should be fine by this evening." Brewer Fester was guaranteed an invite to any event he supplied ale to.

Aquila and Sarra cleared and tidied the table and reset it with fresh bowls and baskets, full of salad leaves and vegetables. They retrieved the geese from the cooking fire, cut them into portions and placed the platters of goose out for guests too.

They supervised the men setting out chairs and benches around the walls of the courtyard under the veranda, and laid blankets over the edge of the veranda, which could also act as seating. Arron was then hailed by a voice from a boat approaching the beach and headed their way.

"You had better get changed if you are going to be ready to greet your guests." Aquila told Sarra, pushing her gently towards her room. "You'll find mine and Papa's gifts in there too."

Sarra went to change and found a fine silvered looking glass standing on her washstand and a new set of silver pins and combs for her hair sitting beside it. One of Aquila's 'errands' on market day had obviously been to Silversmith Staven.

Sarra emerged from her room wearing a new dress of cream linen edged and tied with green, and her hair newly dressed in a coiled plait adorned with silver combs and pins.

Arron called Sarra down to the sea, where a familiar boat was beached, its passengers being helped ashore by her father's friend.

"You know Fisherman Chamo, who lives near the beach north of Corvanna, but I don't think you have met his wife and daughter." Sarra greeted Chamo, her father's tall swarthy friend, who did the introductions:

"This is my wife, Bella and my daughter Sita."

"I am very pleased to meet you." said Bella. "We have brought a platter of large, cooked prawns, but we'll take them up to the house, you had better stay on the beach, there is a small fleet behind us!"

"This is to celebrate your coming-of-age." said Sita, giving Sarra a small gift and a shy smile, before following her mother.

Arron had moved along the beach to greet another boat arriving for the celebration. Sarra was kept busy for a while, greeting guests, all of whom had brought cooked seafoods to add to the feast, along with gifts for herself and some had brought wine too. Arron introduced them all, but there were so many that Sarra knew she would not remember their names.

By the time Arron linked arms with his younger daughter and walked her back to the house, the courtyard was filled with eating, drinking, chattering guests.

Chania put a beaker of wine in Sarra's hand. "You must be the only person here without a drink. I won't bother you with my gift now, you are too busy, and you need to eat too,"

Hetta appeared at Sarra's other side and pressed a roll into her free hand. "I've stuffed it with goose, because most of it had been eaten and you hadn't had as much as a taste."

Sarra realised that she had become quite tired and sat down.

Hetta sat next to her. "I also must thank you for introducing my rolls so many people! I've so many orders for market day, that I am going to have to train someone else up in the baking. I have even met someone, tonight, that is interested in doing that. He name's Jeanni, the wife of Hallon, one of your father's fisher friends. My business is expanding greatly, and I had not even got it set up yet. There is obviously no charge for the fifty rolls your father wanted for tonight. I am obliged to you Sarra. If you set up seriously supplying herbs and the like, you can rely on me to buy them from you, for flavouring my breads and rolls."

Hetta had moved away to talk to others and Sarra found Aunt Kiera by her side.

"Merry nameday to you, Sarra. I've put your clothes and your gift in your room, you are far too busy now." She kissed Sarra lightly on her forehead. "You look lovely. Yanna would have been so proud of her grown-up children. See how handsome Fern has got too."

They looked over to see him laughing and drinking with the fishermen, who always tended to congregate on the beach. Two of the fishermen's daughters, Sita and Dana, were gazing at him in open admiration.

"I know you love growing your plants and have earned coin doing that for a while and that you haven't really had time to think, yet, but if you wanted to apprentice to me and train with Guyon, I would be more than willing. You could still live at home and combine it with any duties you feel you have here. I am hoping that your father might take Trembil as his apprentice, as he has shown an interest and doesn't want to follow Seth into tanning".

Sarra thanked her aunt, but said she needed more time to consider her options, and perhaps her Aunt would care to visit, and bring Trembil, to discuss an apprenticeship, another day.

Sarra got up to circulate amongst the guests, and immediately came across Gemma arguing with Janus. Her voice was getting high and squeaky, which Sarra recognised as anxiety in her friend.

"I'm not saying that you shouldn't be here, I'm just asking who invited you!" her friend insisted. "I'm fairly certain it wouldn't be Sarra or Aquila, so was it Arron or Fern or Sten?"

Janus had turned away from Gemma and her questions with a mumbled "And why wouldn't it be Sarra? We were at school together, the same as you were."

"Because it wasn't the same as me." Gemma retorted. "I was her friend. You were just an irritation!"

"I was her friend." replied Janus, untruthfully. "Anyway, I have a gift for her coming-of-age, and I'm going to be walking out with her."

Sarra was about to turn and walk away from the scene when she saw Wessus place his hand on Janus' shoulder.

"You were never Sarra's friend. She was always kind to everyone, but she was never friends with bullies." Sarra could not walk away now, she was afraid the situation would escalate and spoil the evening.

"I am sure Janus wasn't a bully." she began, trying to keep the peace.

"He was!" broke in Wessus. "He bullied me. He still does! If no-one he cares about is around to see."

Arron suddenly appeared behind Wessus' back. "Good evening, Wessus, Janus, can I get you both a drink of ale? The barrel is near the beach., and where else would it be when there's fisherfolk involved?" He led them away with a hand on the shoulder of each. Janus threw an enraged glance over his shoulder, towards Gemma as he went.

Sarra felt that her head was spinning, with so much going on and so many changes. She needed time to think, to reflect, and to make decisions about her life.

A fiddle suddenly struck up a tune and Sarra followed, with the other guests, towards the music. The evening was a medley of eating, drinking, chatting, and, as time went on, dancing, as everyone ended up on the beach where the fiddler, a drummer and a pipe player collected, and several people sang to their tunes. Sarra was eventually persuaded to bed by Aquila and her Aunt Kiera who promised to return in the morning to help with the clear up.

Sarra woke in the morning with only a fuzzy memory of the later part of the evening. She washed, plaited her hair in a simple long plait, and was reaching for her trews, after all, there was dirty work to be done, when she heard her aunt's voice directing operations. So, instead, she opted for her nearest dress, hitching the skirt up with the belt and covering it with an apron.

The courtyard was a hive of activity when she emerged from her room. Her aunt, Guyon and Aquila were wiping down chairs and benches, which her uncle, father, brother and Sten were then returning to indoor rooms and the storeroom. Even the usual stone courtyard table and benches were getting a wash down and a rub of beeswax. Trembil was on the beach with his brother, Crammer and his younger sister, Hirst, organising a clean-up of anything which did not belong on a beach.

"Sarra, sit down and break your fast." Instructed her Aunt Kera. "Then we can see you open your other gifts, while we take a break and have a drink."

"Yes, sit Sarra, we could do with an excuse for a break. Do not worry about the chickens, they are fed. Though I don't think the goat was overly-impressed by my milking technique." Fern joked.

Sarra sat at the table and was served breakfast by her aunt, while her cousin retrieved several still-wrapped parcels from inside the house.

"I couldn't have waited that long!" insisted Guyor. "I'm dying to know what you've got,"

Sarra unwrapped three pretty scarves in a row. "How many scarves can I wear at once?" she laughed.

"You don't wear them all at once!" her aunt admonished. "It is having a choice that is important."

By the time Sarra had unwrapped her gifts and they had all admired the growing collection of scarves, shawls, necklaces, bracelets, pins and combs that she had, amassed, Kiera had laid out all the leftover seafood and salads for lunch.

Whilst having lunch their conversation had moved on to more serious matters. Guyor and Trembil were twins and had only a few tenights left at school, before looking for work. Guyor had begun to learn weaving from her mother and was happy to continue with that, though, as they only had one loom, this would not mean an increase in production, just possibly some free time for Aunt Kiera.

"It's a good thing I didn't want to take up your offer of an apprenticeship." Sarra said to her aunt. "You would never get any time on the loom yourself!"

Trembil was adamant that he did not want to follow his father's trade of tanning. "Too smelly, and not varied enough." was his pronouncement. He was not expecting the offer from his uncle but was grateful when it came.

"I won't be training Aquila, Fern, Sarra or Sten, they all only want to fish for fun, or when they're hungry, how do you feel about being apprenticed to a fisherman?"

Although he was quite enthusiastic about the idea, Kiera and Seth insisted that Trembil needed time to consider and they would return home for now, but let Arron know very soon.

"You haven't had my present yet." said Sten to Sarra. "It isn't wrapped and it's in the garden."

Sten took Sarra by the hand and walked with her out to the garden. "I'm only glad I didn't get you another scarf or more combs for your hair! I hope you like them."

At the edge of the garden next to the dirt track to town were four huge leafy plants, their roots wrapped in damp sacking, and six large hemispheres of hand-blown glass. "The glass domes are for protecting tender seedlings." explained Sten "And the plants are an exotic fruit called a banana."

"You couldn't have brought me a better present." insisted Sarra, throwing her arms round him and kissing his cheek.

Sarra set to planting the banana plants immediately, with Sten digging four deep holes where Sarra had indicated, at the lower edge of the garden, where they would be protected from wind by the slope and would not shade anything but the chickens, which was a positive outcome of the planting.

While they were in the garden Sarra gathered vegetables to be used for dinner. When Sten and Sarra returned to the others they found that the remains of the pig carcass was being turned into a stew and just needed the vegetables that were in Sarra's hands.

After eating, all four of them agreed that it would be a good idea to catch up on some of the sleep they had missed the previous night.

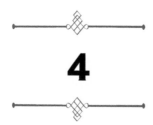

4

The early night they had all had was not reflected in early rising for all of them. Sarra found herself breakfasting alone, despite taking a lot of time to choose her apparel and dress her hair. She eventually decided that dressing up for her family was a waste of time, hitched up her dress, donned an apron and set about her usual chores, starting with the chickens and the goat before moving on to watering the garden.

By the time Sarra returned to the house with salads, Arron had breakfasted, collected mussels, boiled them and the eggs for lunch and was mending his small nets and Aquila was hanging out wet laundry.

Sarra checked the growth of the roots of the plants in cups, while Fern and Sten breakfasted, then she cleared away the breakfast things and set out lunch, before the younger men had moved from the breakfast table.

"Are you chiding us for being slow?" asked Fern.

"No," replied Sarra. "It isn't a market day, so I haven't that chore and I'm just getting ahead, I've run out of chores to complete."

"Excellent!" said Arron, defusing the growing tension. "Then why don't we put the lunch platters into the small nets I've just mended and go on that trip we discussed?"

Fern grinned at his two siblings and gathered up two empty jars to fill with water at the fountain. "Well, no-one's going to ask me twice!"

Sten fetched a jar of wine from the store and five beakers and headed for the boat. Sarra and Aquila slipped the lunch platters with salads into the nets Arron had indicated.

Fern placed the water jars in The Swallow, and he and Arron pushed the boat off the beach into the shallows. Sten waded knee-deep to the boat and passed wine and beakers to Fern before returning to the sands to relieve the girls of the food. He waded out, passed the food to the other men and clambered aboard. The girls hitched up their dresses and walked out to the boat. Fern and Sten took hold of an arm each and hoisted Aquila aboard and then did the same for Sarra. Meanwhile Arron unfurled the sail and then used an oar to push the boat into deeper water.

They passed the morning sailing north, parallel to the reef and its small islands. Several times Arron was hailed by fellow fishermen, but as the day wore on and Corvanna was left further behind, they saw fewer boats.

At one point they found themselves surrounded by disturbed water and Arron could not resist dropping the sail and casting a light net over the side. "We will only be a moment, but the sardines were so near the surface it would have been a crime to leave them there." True to his word the catch was soon hauled aboard, and they were on their way again.

Just as Sarra was about to suggest that they ate their lunch, Arron pointed ahead and said: "There she is: 'Mage's Retreat' on the Isla Grossa!" A large island lay on the horizon. "We'll be there soon."

As they approached it became apparent to Sarra that this isle was composed of the same rock as the reef. They passed it on the left side, but Arron sailed them around the northern side before heading south, up a deeper channel towards a stone-built quay. The wind dropped as they moved into the lee of the cliffs, but Arron looked at the limp sail and it tautened again. The quay itself seemed to be in perfect condition, but the metal ring that Arron tied up to was Verdigris with age. Clambering up the steps, Fern had the girls pass him the food and drink and placed it on a stone table with stone benches beside it.

"Someone has prepared us a feasting table." he jested.

"It was probably used to trade goods." explained Arron. "But the fisherfolk come nowhere near now, not that there is anyone left to trade with."

Sarra set out the food and they poured cups of wine to toast the island's former inhabitants.

They ate and drank as they talked:

"The majority of the buildings are just over the ridge. It's where most of the Elementals and their servants lived, and people with trades worked. It was a whole community and not just a Mage Tower." Arron informed them.

"We have to pass those houses on the way up to the tower, so we'll head that way and look at them first." suggested Arron when they had all finished eating.

The first building they saw on topping the ridge looked almost intact, with just one corner of its slate roof collapsed. When others came into sight, though, they had fared less well, a few being little more than a pile of rubble.

Sten Gasped "The stone has melted there, it's just like lava."

"At least we know there were survivors." said Aquila, indicating a group of crosses grouped on the side of the hill. "People don't usually stay around to bury their enemies!"

"Oh yes." agreed Arron. "There were survivors. I believe they moved to combine with another Tower on an island out on The Greater Sea."

By unsaid common consent they moved uphill towards the graves. Sarra reached the graves first and noticed the initials scrawled on them. "The crosses must have been erected hurriedly, they don't have names on, just initials." she told the others.

Behind the graveyard ran a high wall, broken by a couple of large wooden doors. The group moved towards the nearest door, and finding it unbarred, went through. The space behind the wall was totally enclosed, the high wall forming a boundary to a terraced area of land with a rill of water tumbling down the centre. Next to the entrance were fruit bushes laden with fruit and Sarra reached out and picked some raspberries and ate them. "They are so sweet." she said, with her mouth full. Most of the ground was carpeted with weeds.

"I wonder where the water comes from." said Aquila, heading for the path that climbed the terraces, beside the rill, with a series of steps.

Sarra followed her sister towards the top of the garden for it had obviously been a cultivated area.

At the head of the rill was an overflowing pool. Aquila scooped up some water to drink, then knelt beside it with both hands in the water.

"The water has been raised from deep underground by an Elemental or Elementals working with a Mage. It was difficult to raise but flows freely now."

"How do you know?" Sarra asked.

"I just know." came the answer. Sarra looked at her sister with new respect.

Moving back down the path, Sarra stopped at the first terrace to examine a wooden structure next to the rill. She moved a leaver and watched diverted water run along a smaller channel at the top of the terrace, the water seeping into the soil. She moved the leaver back and the water ceased to flow.

"How clever." she said to Aquila, who had joined her. "I wonder if I could make something like this in our garden. It would make watering so much easier!"

"It would take an awful lot of making." said Aquila. "It would be easier to learn to push the water with your mind!"

"For you!" retorted Sarra. "My plants would wither while they waited."

"It wouldn't actually take long to get this garden sorted, and productive again." Sarra mused, popping a couple of ripe strawberries into her mouth.

"Shall we take a look at the tower?" Sten's voice called across the garden, his main interest in plants was eating them.

The five met up at the gate and, and passing through, walked around the garden wall until the tower came in sight. It was built of reef-rock, as the houses had been, but where they were only one story high, the tower had been hidden by the summit of the island and was the height of at least twelve men.

Sarra stopped to catch her breath. "It is unoccupied?" she whispered.

"It is unoccupied, but not as undamaged as it looks from this side." answered Arron, putting his arm round her shoulder.

They followed the well-worn path as it curved round and approached the tower from the north side. Sarra was shocked to see a gaping hole halfway up the tower and a huge heap of rubble at the base. As they neared the tower they could make out the large recessed arch of the doorway, reaching to twice head height, filled with a substantial wooden door and almost entirely obscured by the rubble which had fallen from above.

"Well, that's the end of that, then!" exclaimed Fern.

"Not necessarily." countered Sten. "I've seen worse falls, and moved worse falls, but it will take time." The others recalled the mining explosions and recovery operations he had talked of.

Arron and Fern moved to the front of the pile and picked up a large stone between them. They sidestepped a couple of lengths with it and set it down.

"No." said Sten. "It's got to be further away, or we'll need a pile that same height too! We will save a lot of time and effort by planning first."

"Sarra, Aquila, did you see any wheelbarrows or carts in the garden?"

"No." replied Sarra. "But there was some sort of shed or store in the lower area." She turned and began walking towards the garden, Aquilla following. "I'll go and look."

Sten called after her: "See if you can find any picks or something to act as a leaver too." He then spoke to Arron and Fern. "This won't be a quick job, we'll either need to leave and come back another day with supplies or, if we stay, break to eat and rest, and possibly sleep, if we want to clear a way in."

"We've the sardine catch in the boat, and a supply of dried biscuits but nothing else. I can catch more fish, but again, that will take time. There are also a couple of blankets and a spare sail in the boat's locker."

"If you two could manage to get those, but don't bother with the sail, I'll go and investigate getting into one of the houses and see what else I can find." Sten was thinking about the rescue teams at the mines, where the whole town worked at supplying them, to keep them working!

Sten turned away to head towards the houses, then turned back. "Bring the water jars and beakers too."

The three men all headed off, Sten striding ahead, but all of them following the downward curving path. As they reached the walled garden, Aquila and Sarra emerged through a door in the wall, each girl pushing a wheelbarrow, Aquila's loaded with two picks and Sarra's with three shovels and a long metal bar.

"Where are you three going, in such a hurry?" Aquila enquired, stopping for a rest.

"Fern and I were heading back to the boat for provisions and blankets, as it looks like a long job, Sten's going to see if he can get into any of the houses, but I can take that off you if you'd prefer." Arron moved towards the wheelbarrow.

"Good idea." said Aquila taking the picks out and propping them against her shoulder. "You'll transport the provisions better in the wheelbarrow."

"That wasn't quite what I meant." protested Arron, but he picked up the wheelbarrow anyway, and using its weight to propel it down the slope, soon caught up with his son.

Sarra came up behind Aquila. "Drop them in here, we'll share the pushing." The two girls took a handle each and pushed the wheelbarrow up the slope.

When Sten reached the first house and rushed to try the first door, he was disappointed to find it locked, but peered inside and was pleased to see two wooden beds with stuffed mattresses, even if there were no blankets. He looked carefully at the window and thought that he could break in if he needed to, though he might wreck the glass in the process. He moved, instead to the next house and discovered that the building was unlocked. Entering, he found himself in a large living room with an eating table and benches in the centre, the room had a large cooking hearth with a chimney and a side oven of the sort usually found in more wealthy houses and several comfortable leather high backed chairs. Through a narrow door, another room contained two large bed frames with straw stuffed mattresses some empty shelving and two cupboards. Returning to the main room, he thought it smelt a little stuffy and opened the shutters to the fresh air. There was no glass at these windows, just one small, glazed window that did not open. He smiled at the thought that the owner knew that there was no point in locking a door when the shuttered windows gave such easy access.

With the light flowing in, he noticed an oil lamp hanging from a central beam, which, when he shook it, proved to still contain lamp oil.

Leaving the house, he saw Fern returning with the carry-nets containing platters, jars and beakers. He waved him over and suggested leaving most in the house, just re-filling the jars from the stream in the garden, to take to the tower base with the beakers.

"If you wait here and gather what wood you can find and some of the dried grass there is near the houses, for kindling, you could stop Arron from bringing the fish and the blankets any further, we can cook and camp out here, then you could both come up with the wheelbarrow, I'll fill the jars and take them up and make a start with the girls."

By the time Arron and Fern arrived back at the tower Aquila, Sarra and Sten had shovelled and barrowed a large heap of loose rubble some distance from the tower. Seeing the arrival of the two relatively fresh men the girls handed over their shovels and proposed taking the water jars to the garden for a refill. They did not mention their intention to rinse the dirt and sweat away while they were there.

Sarra and Aquila arrived back at the tower with re-filled water jars, refreshed and damp, unfortunately this encouraged the dirt to stick to their skin, soon making them dirtier than before.

They worked steadily through the afternoon. Sten was about to suggest that they might be able to squeeze past the remainder of the pile and open the door, when Arron reminded them that they had to collect fuel and light a fire before they could cook fish for dinner, and that the fish needed gutting and skewering.

The girls collected an armful of wood and twigs on the way back to the abandoned village and claimed first rights to the rill to clean up. They entered the unlocked house and dropped the fuel on the hearth, before heading for the walled garden. Sten and Arron collected more fuel while Fern entered the house with a handful of dried grasses tied into a ball and placed it in the fireplace. He was tired from the physical exertion, and it took a couple of minutes concentration before a wisp of smoke and then a tiny flame escaped the tinder. Fern fed the fire with the fuel the girls had brought, then, when Arron and Sten arrived with more fuel, left them to tend the fire while he went to clean the fish.

The girls brought the cleaned fish in to cook, cleaner than they had been, but bemoaning the lack of soap. They took over the fire area and sent the men to clean themselves. The men returned quickly, and they all ate the sardines straight from the skewers, burning fingers and lips in the process. There were a few salad leaves left from lunch to eat with them, as well as the dried biscuits but Sarra was sobered by the thought that there would only be sardines for breakfast, and there would be no-one at home in the morning to feed the chickens or milk Hella.

They were all tired and agreed on an early night. The men went to take a brief look at the other houses before it got too dark. The girls lit the lamp from the remains of the fire and spread the two blankets over the two mattresses. They sat on the benches at the table and speculated as to what the tower would hold.

When the men returned, Aquila was standing behind Sarra, combing her hair with one of her small silver combs, before arranging it in a loose plait and retying the ends. The girls then swapped places and Sarra did the same for Aquila. Arron suggested they take the lamp for the other room and that the four should share the two beds. He had the light of the fire and would sleep in a chair.

The girls took one bed and the boys took the other, the girls and Fern quickly fell asleep, but Sten lay listening to the others breathing slow, and pondered on what the next day would reveal.

Sarra felt disorientated when she woke, her cheek against the rough sisal weave of the mattress. She slipped out of bed without disturbing Aquila, stole through the door and came face to face with Fern, entering the house with an armful of fuel. Sarra put her finger to her lips to indicate that the others were still asleep then whispered to Fern: "I can't face fish for breakfast, I'm going to see what fruit I can find in the garden. She picked up the three empty platters in carrying nets and left.

Sarra's entry to the garden disturbed a flock of birds on nearby bushes, so she went to investigate there first and found large, blue-black berries with a bloom on them. She picked one and tasted it. It seemed tart initially, but melted into sweetness, so she tried a second. The second seemed even sweeter than the first, so she put down the carry nets and began picking in earnest. When she had stripped the bushes, she went searching to see what else she could find. Sarra wandered about the garden, seeing many familiar plants, which had either been perennials or plants self-set from annual food crops. She was just adding perennial herbs to a platter of salad leaves, when she heard her father calling her name.

"Good morning, father, did you sleep alright in the chair?" she asked, joining him by the rill.

"I woke with a slightly crooked neck, but slept all night, sound enough to not hear you rise."

"I came out to find fruit for breakfast and I have two platters full of raspberries, strawberries, a black berry I don't know, and peaches and apricots. I also have a platter of salad leaves and herbs for lunch with the sardines." Sarra said with satisfaction.

"Wonderful, no-one knows their plants better than you. I am refilling the water jars so we can refresh ourselves and get back to the tower. I think we will be able to get in without moving too much more rubble."

When Arron and Sarra returned to the house, the others were just getting ready to leave for the tower but turned back when they saw the fruit. They made a good breakfast from all the gathered fruit.

On returning to the tower, they decided there was room enough to enter. Arron manoeuvred past the rubble and pushed open the heavy oak door.

"Dusty, but passable. No rubble inside." came Arron's verdict. "In you come." he invited.

They did not have to be asked twice and hurried into the tower. The entire ground floor was open to them, a high-ceilinged room furnished with comfortable high-backed leather chairs, similar to the one Arron had slept in, leather sofas, and low tables. There were glazed windows high in the wall, providing light, but not views or air. On one side was a circular stone trough with a pump handle beside it, and on the other side a wide staircase hugged the wall and disappeared through a hole in the ceiling.

Aquila crossed the room and worked the pump handle producing a rush of water, which she caught in her cupped hand and tasted.

43

"No trips back to the rill from here then!" she said with satisfaction.

Fern put the beakers and water jugs on the table nearest to the trough. "That suits me!"

With unspoken consensus they together mounted the stairs to the floor above. The floor above contained an open area where the stairs continued to spiral up the wall and a wooden partition with two doors. Sten moved to the first door and opened it wide so they could all step inside. The room was lit by two glazed windows and had a smaller unglazed shuttered window. It contained two tables and four hard, high-backed chairs. The stone walls were lined with empty shelves. They exited the room and went through the other door. They were met with a similar room, again with two glazed windows and one shuttered one, this time containing a table, two high-backed chairs and three stools. The shelves here were narrow shelves, divided vertically as well as horizontally, but much deeper. Sarra looked at them in puzzlement and turned towards Fern.

"Scroll racks." he answered, before she had even put the question.

"Perhaps there will be something of more interest on the next floor." said Sten, dejectedly. "I thought there would be more left than this. Something that told us about their work, or their way of life would be good."

"There are more floors above us, there may be something there." Aquila said cheerfully.

"Anyway," said Arron, with caution. "I don't want to find anything too exciting. Exciting can mean dangerous, where Mages are concerned!"

"We've got a long way to go yet, judging by the height of this tower. Let's try the next floor." said Fern, heading for the stairs.

They mounted the stairs with differing amounts of enthusiasm, but what met them at the top was quite different to the layout on the floors below. There were no separate rooms, but partitions had been erected perpendicular to the walls, creating five open 'bays', each one with a glazed window and with shelving from floor to ceiling on the three 'bay' walls. Rather than being empty, as they had been in the rooms below, these shelves were crammed full of glass stoppered jars of various sizes, containing animals, plants, and parts of animals, all in a clear, viscus liquid.

"Is this more to your liking?" Fern asked Sten,

"I'm not sure." said Sten, placing a jar containing a newly hatched chicken back on the shelf, on the exact spot he had removed it from. He looked round to see what the others were doing and found Sarra kneeling on the floor in front of shelves full of preserved plant material.

"So many plants!" she said in wonder. "So many plants I've never seen before, and berries and fruits…"

Sten offered her his hand and helped her to her feet. "There isn't time to look at them all now." he said.

"Why not?" Sarra asked.

Sten gestured to the stairs, where Arron and Aquila were already making their way up to the next floor.

"They are just impatient!" bemoaned Sarra.

Following on, they found an open area again with no partitioning walls at all, furnished with comfortable high-backed leather chairs and around a large circular table. Arron and Aquila were already making use of two of the chairs, so Sarra, Fern and Sten joined them.

"Time to take stock." announced Arron. "It would take Sarra, at least, days to look properly at that store of specimens. We have already spent one night here. No-one knows where we are, the chickens haven't been fed or the goat milked. Do we head back now, prepare better and come back tomorrow? Do we risk worrying relatives and possibly sacrificing the chickens and goat by extending our stay and exploring thoroughly? Or do we compromise by having a quick look at each floor before heading home, then returning later for a real appraisal?

Sarra was the first to express an opinion. "Letting the chickens and goats to suffer is not an option!"

"There are other options." offered Aquila, always the peacemaker. "You and I could go back, Father, and take care of the chickens and Hella. The chickens could range free for a few days – they will not go far, they know Sarra looks after them, even if she steals their eggs! We could bring Hella back with us and have fresh milk. We could bring provisions and clean clothes and blankets. Sarra could forage in the garden until tomorrow, Sarra could examine the specimens and Fern and Sten could explore the other houses. We could leave now and be back before sunset. Then we could all explore the rest of the tower."

Fern was quick to object to his sister's plan: "So we have to wait, and not explore the tower, just because you aren't here? We can explore the other houses? Thank you very much for that! It's kind of you to allow us that!"

Sten tried to smooth things over: "It's only natural that Aquila wants to explore the tower with us." he stated. "I would suggest that we do as Arron first suggested and take a quick look at each floor and then decide if we should all go back, or to split the group temporarily."

"Excellent!" said Arron. "Well, I'm glad we're all in agreement!"

He got to his feet ignoring two shocked and two puzzled faces and made for the stairs. The four younger members of the party leapt to their feet and hurried to join him. At the top of the stairs they found another unpartitioned room with lots of shelving containing similar glass jars to before, with glass stoppers and labels. These seemed, at the quick glance they were given, to mostly contain coloured powders and liquids and, to Sarra's disappointment, no specimens at all. A large table to one side was covered in apparatus in glass and metal, that Sarra could make no sense of at all.

"Alchemy!" muttered Sten, before following Arron up the next set of stairs.

Sarra was very surprised, on reaching the next floor, to see that the stairs continued. She had expected to have reached the top floor by now. The floor was, again, an open area, though each floor had got smaller as they had climbed the tower. There were tables below the glazed windows with shelving on the walls, on the tables were quill pens and bottles containing dried up ink. A sheaf of new parchment sheets sat waiting on one of the tables. Aquila and Fern had now joined them, so they all headed up the stairs together, to the next floor.

The light that met them there was tremendous. There were glazed windows looking out in every direction. When their eyes had adjusted, they realised that the whole of this top floor was taken up with a huge table covered with what appeared to be a painted representation of The Little Sea.

Sarra gasped. "Look at the way it's done, you can even see the shallow water near the shore and between the islands of the reef! Look at the little model boats. Doesn't that one in The Great Sea look like Chamo's Seaspray? it's the only boat that is painted red that I know of." she reached out a hand.

"No!" Yelled Arron and Sten together.

"You can't touch it." Sten added.

Aquila moved closer to the table, "Look there's Torroja." She said pointing near the edge of the map. "There is Corvanna." she added pointing near the other edge. "There's Janus' farmhouse, but it is as big as it is now, and he only enlarged it last year!"

Both sisters bent over the table to examine the detail.

Sarra was mesmerised. "Look at the island, it's so realistic, it's even got the terraced garden and the little houses and the tower." She peered closer at the Isla Grossa. "It's got the rubble piled up near the base, but it's where we put it, not where it was, against the tower, how did they know we were going to put it there? And the door is half open too." She took another shallow breath. "The boat tied up at the quay, I'd swear it was The Swallow."

She had reached out and picked up the model boat before anyone could stop her or speak. As she picked it up the rope, thin as a linen thread taughtened, then the ring the rope was tied to, pulled out of, and then dropped onto, the quay, parting the rope. Her nail tore through the fabric of the sail, so she rather guiltily, put it back on the water next to the quay.

"No!" Screamed Aquila.

Arron grabbed Sarra's arms and held them by her side so that she could not reach forward again.

Sten ran for the stairs.

"Quick Fern, we've got to tie her up again and stop her drifting away!" Fern fled down the stairs after him.

"What is he talking about, Papa? What is going on? What happened? Where have they gone?"

Arron didn't want her to panic, so spoke as calmly as he could. "They've just gone down to The Swallow, to tie her up and make sure she doesn't drift away and leave us here, marooned."

"Why would she drift away? She's tied up at the quay."

"She was tied up Sarra. I do not know how you could touch anything on the map, it is a Mage's Map, and you shouldn't have been able to touch it. It is protected by magic. But you moved Swallow and the rope pulled out the ring it was tied to. Let's follow them down and check everything's alright."

5

Arron led Sarra down the stairs still holding her hand, Aquila following.

Arron was practically running down the stairs and when they reached the bottom, Sarra stopped to catch her breath. Aquila picked up the water jar and beakers and rushed to the door.

"To the boat, Sarra. It's interesting here, but I wouldn't want to be stranded!"

Aquila and Sarra squeezed past the door and into the open air. Arron was already rushing down the pathway towards the walled garden. Aquila pulled the door closed, behind them, then wondered who she was shutting out. The two girls ran on after him, trying to catch up, past the garden, through the cluster of houses and towards the quay.

Before they reached the quay, as the sea came clearly into sight, Sarra stopped, her hands to her mouth in horror.

The Swallow, bobbed on the sea, her torn sail dangling from the mast, and hanging over the side of the boat, dragging in the sea as she drifted. She had drifted away from the island towards the lagoon, but fortunately not too far. Two heads bobbed in the water, one dark and one red-haired, swimming towards the boat. Fern reached the boat first, hauling himself aboard, then helped Sten to get aboard. They pulled the tattered sail out of the water, then shipped the oars. By the time they had turned the boat about and rowed her back to the quay, Arron was waiting to catch the rope and pull Swallow in, to the quayside.

Sarra sat on the stone bench she had sat on so happily yesterday, looking stricken. She looked up at her dripping brother with tear filled eyes.

"Did I do that to The Swallow?" she asked. "I would never harm Papa's boat! It's just not possible!"

"We all know that." replied her brother as calmly as he could. "We all know you wouldn't damage Swallow. And we know what you did is not possible. We also know it happened. Now let us go home."

Sarra took her brother's proffered hand and he led her to the boat. She could not meet her father's eyes, although she knew he was watching her. Sarra settled herself in the stern, out of the way. Sten had already removed the spare sail from the locker, and he and Arron set about removing the damaged sail and replacing it. When it was in position and raised, Arron sailed Swallow out of the inlet and out into the lagoon. He then handed the tiller over to Fern and settled himself on the seat beside his younger daughter. He wrapped his arms around Sarra and held her close.

"It's alright, there's no real harm done, we're all safe and sound and on our way home." He kissed Sarra's forehead. "It shouldn't have been possible. I've never worked with a Mage Map, although I know Fern and Sten have. If we had thought there was any danger, we'd have kept you from it, you know that."

At his gentle cajoling, she relaxed in his arms as she had as a child. He continued to talk to her, his gentle voice soothing her. "We'll go straight home and tend to Hella and the chickens. You can work in the garden, and I'll get us some fish for lunch. Aquila will go into town and get some provisions, and in the morning Fern and Sten will go off to see the Mages and sort all of this out. You may need to go to Mage College to see the Mages, but that will take time and, in the meanwhile, you can attend to the garden and the house and I won't leave the Little Sea. The Great Sea and the fish there will just have to wait for me. Well, until after I have got another spare sail, anyway! Things could have been worse! You could have dropped her and broken the keel!"

Arron's attempt at humour brought a fresh bout of tears.

Aquila gave her father a stern look and took his place.

"It's all going to be alright, Sarra. It is just a shock to you. There were we trying to tell you how you might find magic, or how magic might find you, and you took a different route."

Sarra's tear filled eyes met her sister's. "You think that was magic?"

"Well, I don't know any other way of lifting a model boat from a map and moving a real one, do you?" Sarra did not answer, but just stared deep into the water rushing past. She lifted her eyes to meet Aquila's. "What will happen now?" she eventually asked.

"Like Papa said, we'll go home and tend to necessary chores, I'll go into town and order a new sail and get travelling food, and tomorrow Fern and Sten will head off to Mage College to talk to them about what happened."

Aquila paused. "I would imagine they'll want you to go to Mage College, so we will assume that is the case and get you ready and equipped, but until they tell us that is the case, we will all stay close to home, with you, and things will continue as normal."

Aquila looked at her father, brother and his friend to check that they were listening. "Until a Mage tells us differently, we'll say nothing of what happened here, we will keep it between the five of us. However, we do need put arrangements in place for you to leave for Mage College as soon as you are called to."

Sarra leaned her head on her sister's shoulder and just wished she was back home now.

Sarra must have been half asleep, because in no time at all, it seemed, the Swallow's keel scraped on the shingle beach and came to rest. Arron jumped out of the boat, up to his knees in water, took Sarra into his arms and carried her up the beach.

"It's alright, Papa, I can walk." but her protestations were in vain.

"You're still in shock, Sarra. You need to rest, and after that you will probably need to eat."

Sarra was tired, she admitted that to herself, though she did not know why she should be. Her sense of duty still won out: "I have to go to Hella, she will be swollen and getting sore."

Arron continued to Sarra's room and placed her down on the bed. "Aquila's already gone to her. You are not used to using magic yet, it's going to tire you, deplete your body, you're going to need to rest and to eat, not always in that order! You were practically asleep in the boat coming home. Now rest, there'll be food when you wake, and we can talk then."

"I'll feed the chickens" Arron insisted, when Sarra started to rise.

Sarra lay back on her bed, in the comfort of being home, in her own room, and slept.

Sarra woke, stretched, listened to her stomach rumble and realised that she was ravenous.

Outside, as she passed under the veranda, the smell of seared prawns and saffron infused fish stew met her and drew her to the table. Fern and Sten were dipping chunks of bread into their bowls and Sarra, who couldn't wait for her bowl to be filled, dipped a chunk of bread in her father's bowl and wolfed it down.

Arron ladled stew into an empty bowl and set it in front of his daughter.

"I'd like to keep my own lunch! It's been an eventful day!" he joked.

In the centre of the table sat the bronze ring that had tethered Swallow to the quay. A lump of mortar surrounded the pin that had secured it to the dock.

Sarra spooned stew into her mouth but picked up the ring in her other hand. "I thought it had pulled out of its hole." she said, when her mouth was empty for long enough to speak.

"No." said Sten slowly. "That wouldn't be strong enough to hold larger boats to the quay in a storm, even in the lee of the inlet. The rings are always Mage forged into the quays, to make sure they hold."

"But it didn't hold." pointed out Sarra.

"That was exactly what we were saying." said Fern.

"How can that be?" asked Sarra.

"That is the real question" agreed Sten.

"If it's Mage forged, it can only be Mage destroyed." said Sten emphatically.

"Then there must have been a Mage on the island." Sarra's logic was sound.

"Exactly!" agreed Fern.

"Do you think he was hiding in one of the houses?" Sarra was still eating as she talked and helped herself to the last of the bread.

"There's some rolls inside if you are still hungry." said Aquila, topping up her sister's bowl. "They were for tomorrow, but I could fetch more."

"You've been to town already?" Sarra's guilt kicked in again.

"Only to the Brewer, and Baker, and Chandler and Aunt Kiera's. Nowhere interesting." Aquila tried to reassure her.

Fern broke into their conversation, annoyed that the line of thought and talk had been diverted: "Sarra! Mages don't hide! They insist! They demand! They rage! They compel! BUT THEY DO NOT HIDE!!"

"But you agreed that there had to be a Mage on the island. I didn't see anyone there but the five of us." Sarra was confused.

Arron laid a hand on his son's arm. "Gently, Fern." he admonished. "Sarra is tired and stressed."

"Yes, father, but she has to understand what happened, too." Fern was unbowed.

"Sarra, none of us saw anyone else on the island." Fern spoke slowly and gently, now. "There wasn't anyone else there."

"But..." began Sarra, but there was no other thought following it.

"Sarra, were you doing anything as we sailed back home?" asked her father.

"No, I was too tired. What sort of anything?" she questioned. "I was just upset at damaging Swallow and wishing we could be home as fast as possible." she added.

The other four exchanged glances.

Sten took Sarra's hand. "Sarra, we know you used magic on the island, but we aren't absolutely sure what kind of magic, yet. Can we all try some experiments with you, later, when you have your strength back."

"Yes, of course. I'm quite eager to know where my affinity lies, myself."

Sarra felt restless, but Aquila had taken over the chores that needed doing, so Sarra wandered out to the garden and hoed a few weeds, before picking salad leaves to accompany their next meal. She surveyed her domain and the stream running through the garden. She considered how much time and effort it would take to terrace the slope, and whether she could persuade Fern and Sten to make her enough open clay piping with seepage holes to irrigate the garden, and how much coin she would need to earn in order to pay the carpenter to construct enough lever worked paddles for each level. She would have to grow a lot of plants to sell at market, this year, and approach Carpenter Daffid next year, she thought, but meanwhile would begin on the terraces as she cleared the ground of crops.

Sarra returned to the courtyard to cook the evening meal.

"Omelettes for everyone?" she asked cheerfully, on her return, ignoring the muted discussion which had silenced on her arrival.

"Would you like me…" Fern indicated the cooking fire laid ready to be used. But before she had time to voice her agreement, it burst into flame.

"Thank you, Fern." Sarra said cheerfully.

"That's me! Done!" Fern said to Aquila and Sten.

Aquila took a water jug, filled it at the fountain and set it and beakers on the table. She then took a clay matrix that Fern and Sten had made for them and set it beside the jug, filling it with water.

"Would you like…?" Aquila asked as Sarra looked down at it.

Sarra smiled. "Ice would be wonderful, if you're not too tired."

The water turned to ice as the two watched, and Aquila tipped it into the water jar.

"No problem at all!" Aquila nodded at Fern and raised an eyebrow at Sten.

Sten spoke to them in a whisper: "Earth would be more difficult and would have to wait until another day. I have seen everything I need to, to be convinced, and I think Arron has too. We just need to talk to her now and inform the Mages at the College.'"

"As soon as possible, I think." agreed Arron.

"I will stay here while she is away at College." volunteered Aquila.

"There is no need, I am not a child, I can manage alone, and Kiera will help if I need it." insisted Arron.

Sarra laid omelettes filled with vegetables on platters on the table and called them to eat. Arron fetched a jar of wine and poured out five cups.

"Did we not drink enough the other night, Papa?" Sarra enquired.

"That was to celebrate your nameday, and your coming of age." Arron stated firmly, raising his cup to Sarra. "Today we have something different to celebrate."

"What is that Papa?" she asked.

"Arron took a mouthful of his meal, chewed and swallowed before answering. "Today we celebrate the talent of my younger daughter."

"The chickens produced the eggs, Papa, a much cleverer thing than me cooking them."

"Not that talent, Sarra, the one that allowed you to manipulate a Mage Map, a feat you should not have been able to accomplish."

Sarra coloured. "I moved a model boat, Papa!"

"You only saw what happened in the tower, Sarra, and the results at the quayside. We did not see the reality of it! You lifted a boat out of the water, high enough to pull the rope, you damaged a Mage Forged quay and tore a good quality sail with your fingernail! Can you imagine what that would have looked like to someone standing on the quay-side?"

Sarra stared at her father open-mouthed, she went white and then burst into tears.

Sten moved next to her and placed an arm round her shoulder.

"Arron isn't expressing himself very well." began Sten. "No ordinary person could have moved anything on that map table. It is designed to help a Mage and his Elementals effect great feats of magic in the real world by focusing the Elemental power through the map. Few Mages can do that. You didn't even do it with the help of Affines acting as your Elementals, - you did it alone!"

Sten took a breath and continued. "Since then, you have also shown that you can enhance the work of Affines, using them like Elementals. You helped Arron produce a strong, true, wind to get us home quickly. Arron has said that he has never covered that distance as quickly before. You helped Fern light the cooking fire."

Sarra looked at her brother.

He shrugged. "I'm quick, but I'm not that quick!"

"Then you helped Aquila produce ice in record time. You did not even do these things consciously; you just knew they were going to try to do these things and aided them.

Sarra turned to look at Sten. "I think I need to go to bed." she said.

Sarra emptied her cup with one swallow, kissed Arron goodnight, blew a kiss to Fern and Aquila and made for her room.

"Goodnight, Sarra." whispered Sten quietly.

6

Sarra was awake early and felt too restless to stay in bed. She dressed in trews and tunic and made her way through the garden to the chickens and goats. She walked beside the stream that rose as a spring in the goat's enclosure, then ran through the chicken run, providing them with water, then on through the garden in its turn providing water for the plants. As she walked up the slope of the garden, she recalled her thoughts of the previous day. She had been planning how she would, over time, terrace the garden; turn the stream into a tumbling rill, constrained by the straight edges of slates; watering the tiers she would create in the garden, with the lift of a paddle. It would take a long time to achieve but would allow much more to be grown in terms of seedlings and crops for market and providing her with enough coin, from doing a job she loved. This was time that she now would not have. She would have no time to do the job as she did it now, or to make the improvements that she wanted to make, which would save time. There would be no time for that now if she had to go to Mage College. She should be pleased, she had been longing to discover an affinity, but the discovery that she may be a latent Mage nudged her to the edge of panic. She was no longer in charge of her own destiny.

In the past few days she had seen her ideal life present itself, then become impossible to achieve. She had moved from being a child with no vision of her future, to a woman with a dream, and then to a woman with no vision of the future again.

She returned to her room and changed into a dress.

As she moved out into the courtyard, she recalled her father saying, just a few days ago that she had lots of futures to choose from, but then she remembered Sten saying that once magic had chosen you, there were no choices. Sten sat alone at the table having a breakfast that he must have set.

She greeted him with the brightest smile she could manage. "Tell me about Mage College" she asked.

"About Mage College in general, or about my experience of it?" Sten asked.

"Both." she replied.

"I'll begin at the beginning, then. Originally the Mage's ran the College to develop the skills of those with an affinity for the four elements, either to be used on their own, as Affines or to become Elementals to the Mages, or, if they were strong enough, to become Mages in their own right. So that each Mage could build their own power base in a Tower, or establish a community based on magic, hiring themselves out on commissions. They also gave Affines and Mages a much wider education as well as focusing on magic."

"These days there are few Mages, so the College is run by senior officials, on loan from the King, and just a few Mages. The Mages there develop the skills of groups of Affines who have an affinity for a particular element, working in groups with one affinity to boost their power, or sometimes across disciplines. If you go to Mage College as a latent Mage, you will almost certainly be working with the Mages and probably with groups of Affines to learn how to enhance their skills and make them more powerful. But we already know that you can do that for Affines of three elements - even if it is ones that you are close to. We can test your influence on my affinity if you want to?" Sten Grinned at her, and then moved on: "You will probably be encouraged to form a Tower or a community with unattached Affines, since there are so few Mages left. You could then take on commissions as a group to earn coin collectively or live as a community to do things for yourselves. Most communities have servants with them who aren't magical."

"When Fern and I were at college together we found that we worked well together on joint projects, earth and fire often does, but we dreamed of finding a latent Mage and setting up a community. Even when we've worked together on commissions since, we always dreamt of finding a Mage and becoming Elementals. It's one reason we wanted to go to the island – to look for anything that would give a clue to how they achieved what they achieved. And there you were, with us all the time!"

Sten ladled yoghurt and honey into a bowl.

"Eat. You need to keep your strength up. Magic is depleting."

Then he continued, watching to make sure she ate: "You have a ready-made team of Affines to become your Elementals, if that is what you decide you want to do. One Affine of each element as your first Elementals, three of whom you are related to who would never let you down – and I wouldn't either – with you I would achieve my dream. Not that I would want to influence you, of course!"

"They will – the College, that is! They might want you to form a team to work for the College; or to form a Tower in the capital, working for the King; or one of the provincial cities. They may even want you to teach at Mage College. You have to remember that there is a great shortage of Mages, they will want you working as soon as possible."

"Whatever happens you must learn all you can and not commit yourself too early, and finally, after training, have a long rest, and then decide what YOU want to do. And if you are ever in need of an earth Elemental, I'm your man! Fern will be desperate to be a fire Elemental for you, and I can't see Aquila or Arron wanting to cut you adrift. So, my advice would be to go to Mage College, to learn everything they can teach you, keep an open mind and then YOU decide." Sten loosened his grip on Sarra's hand. "Eat!"

"So, I don't have to live in a Tower?"

"No, no, no!" Sten nearly choked on his breakfast. "Live in a Tower; stay at Mage College and help Affines there; move to court and work for the King; make a community for yourself here – it's all up to you! There will be almost nothing you can't do once you're a Mage and you've finished your training."

"You're sure I'm going to be a Mage?"

"Absolutely!"

"You're sure they'll want me at Mage College?" Sarra still did not really believe it.

"When Fern and I tell them what you are capable of, completely untrained, they will be hammering on your father's door, demanding that you go!"

This did not cheer Sarra.

"Who will tend the garden and milk the goat while I'm gone? Who will look after Papa?"

"Arron said he can manage alone, but once we've told the College about you and come back, Fern and I have no commissions planned. Neither has Aquila at the moment, so we can be here. Mage College will pay you, or employ someone in your place, while you train. You'll be training on commissions, so earning for the College."

"Fern and I will go to Mage College today, we can be back in three or four days, then we will stay here, if that is what you want."

Fern appeared behind Sten, nodding in agreement, before helping himself to breakfast.

Sarra pushed her bowl away and smiled her first real smile that morning. "Alright, you've convinced me. You had better go see if they want me."

When Aquila and Arron joined them, they discussed the logistics of that decision:

Sten and Fern would leave before noon and be at the College the next day. Since it was a journey Sten and Fern did often, they knew of a lodging house at the right distance to spend the night. They might be able to see a Mage the day that they arrived and convey the news, but if not, the following day, so they should be back on the third or fourth day, the fifth at the most.

When each of them found an affinity and were called to go to Mage College, they went within a tenight, so this was the timescale that Sarra should work to. She made a list as thy talked, she would need a stout pair of walking shoes for travelling long distance; new sandals and slippers for indoors; the fare for using a cart on the highway; a travelling cloak; she could use Aquila's travelling bag, as she would stay at home; four dresses besides the one she wore; five sets of underthings; sleeping tunics and writing materials as well as personal items. She should not need much more coin as everything else would be taken care of by the College.

It was planned that Aquila would take over the garden, so, as she was less adept with the plants and animals, she should simplify this where possible; Sarra should check on the health of the beehives before leaving; she would sow crops of salad leaves and beans for winter-keeping; sow winter roots; and Sarra should sell her stock of seedlings. Aquila could arrange to keep things weed free and harvest crops, even taking excess to market, along with Arron's fish. Aquila did not worry about such tasks being below the notice of an Affine, though Sarra did. Arron planned to do one deep-water trip into The Great Sea before Sarra left, then he would stick to more local trips in The Little Sea, or just the other side of the reef, while Sarra was away. Aquila and Fern would take local commissions only, though Sten might work further away.

With all this settled, Sarra and Aquila prepared travelling food while Sten and Fern packed light travelling packs, and then set off.

Arron removed the torn sail from Swallow's locker and replaced it with the one Aquila had got from the chandler's the previous day. He pushed the boat into the shallows, and with a wave of his hand, headed off for the Deep Channel to The Great Sea.

Sarra and Aquila headed for the garden. Sarra talked Aquila through what she was currently growing and what she was planning. There would be a market tomorrow, so they should prepare the seedlings to be ready for taking to market that afternoon. Watering everything first, they decided that harvesting courgettes and beans to take to market, should be their other priority.

"I can harvest salad crops from these two sections for us tomorrow, then, after we return from the market they can be cleared and replanted with salads and roots." Sarra told her sister.

Aquila gave Sarra's hand a squeeze. "It's alright, Sarra, you don't have to plan everything, we'll muddle through, and even if we make mistakes, it won't really matter, we won't starve. Anyway, you won't really be gone that long."

Arron didn't return that evening and Sarra and Aquila ate a lone meal, followed by ripe figs and a cup of wine. They went to bed tired and relaxed, knowing they have achieved much.

Sarra woke early the next day and had milked the goat and breakfasted when Aquila rose.

Sarra was harvesting salad leaves into a carry-basket when Aquila arrived at the garden with another large carry basket and two carry nets containing courgettes and beans harvested the previous day.

"There will be other markets, Sarra, and we have coin for the things you need. This is as much as we can carry into town."

They set off for Corvanna with their baskets and nets, arriving not long after the market opened. Aquila spread her cloak on the ground, and they sat on it, arranging their wares around themselves.

They were selling well when Katerina approached Sarra.

"Have you no plants for sale this morning, Sarra?"

"No. I have seedlings to sell, but we couldn't carry them today. I'll probably have them here at next market day" Sarra said.

"Or you could collect them, for a discount." suggested Aquila.

"You'll have to get Arron to buy a donkey and cart, if you keep growing so much." said Katerina.

"Sarra may not need that if she goes to Mage College soon." interrupted Aquila.

"Is that likely?" asked Katerina, and at Aquila's nod continued: "Then I'd better collect the plants I need while the opportunity is still there. Would tomorrow morning be convenient? My husband won't need the cart then."

It was agreed that the next morning would be fine for collection.

A short while later, they were approached by another regular buyer, Tanner Corbin's wife, Hannish, asking if she could collect seedling plants in the morning too, while they were still available.

"News travels fast!" remarked Aquila to her sister.

They had sold most of their produce when other venders began packing their wares away. Aquila packed what was left into one basket, stacked the others, with nets inside, and when Sarra stood up, shook out her cloak.

"Aunt Kiera first, I think." she said, leading the way.

Stepping into the cool interior of Aunt Kiera's house, they found her, as usual, at her loom.

"Aquila, Sarra, I was just thinking of you. I did not get time to go to market this morning, but I was wondering if you were there. What a great celebration we had! How Yanna would have laughed to think that her baby daughter had come-of-age! This length is one that Arron commissioned for you, would you prefer a yellow, or rust border?" She gestured to the long length of cream linen on the loom.

"We have more to celebrate now, Aunt." Aquila broke in.

"Another celebration? Don't tell me that charming friend of your brother's has offered marriage to one of my nieces?" Kiera peered from one blushing face to the other as she waited for an answer.

Aquila put her right: "No, nothing like that! Fern and Sten have gone off to Mage College with news, and we are expecting them to return with an invitation for Sarra."

"So Sarra, you have an affinity too? You are a family well blessed, though it is to be expected of a family of Arron and Yana, is it not?"

Sarra avoided the first question. "Yes, I suppose it is a blessing, but leaving Papa will be a wrench."

"If Arron needs help in the house or the garden, or going to market, Guyor will be looking for work, she is a strong and willing girl."

"I thought she was to learn weaving, as your apprentice?" questioned Sarra.

"Yes." replied Aunt Kiera. "But as we only have one loom, we will both have quite a lot of free time to occupy, and Guyor thought she might try to get other work, to earn coin and save for a loom."

"I will mention that to Papa." said Aquila. "Though I will be around for a while, and we don't know when Sarra will be called yet."

Aquila laid down the basket she was carrying. "Can you use these vegetables, Aunt? We called also because we must commission more garments for Sarra, for when she is called to Mage College. She will need more underthings and sleeping tunics, and we don't want to send her with the bare minimum."

They spent a while with Aunt Kiera discussing Sarra's garment requirements, over some of the food they had brought and a small goat's cheese, before taking themselves off to complete their commissions.

Near to Aunt Kiera's house they called at a workshop sporting the sign of a large shoe.

The bent, elderly cobbler met them at the entrance and introduced himself to Sarra as Cobbler Fendi. "Of course, I know your sister well, I made her boots and sandals to go to Mage College and have kept then in repair ever since, and your brother too, of course. If that father of yours ever buys a donkey and cart, half my trade will go!" Fendi laughed at his own joke.

"In that case, I've bad news for you!" Aquila joked back. "But we do need a stout pair of black walking boots for Sarra, along with a new pair of lace-up sandals and a pair of soft kid indoor slippers."

"Ah, she'll be following in your footsteps then, young Aquila?"

"It rather looks that way, Cobbler Fendi." Aquila replied with a smile.

Fendi took the measurements of Sarra's feet, then brought out kid skins for their inspection. "The boots will be strong cows' leather, in black, for good wear, the sandals a similar leather in tan, with tan thongs to tie, but you have the choice of colour for the slippers. Your Uncle Seth is producing some kid in lovely colours for the ladies, these days." There were yellow, russet, blue and green skins there, along with the more common black, brown and tan. Sarra chose the green.

Aquila paid Cobbler Fendi with several silver coins taken from a drawstring purse, winking at Sarra as she did so. "Papa was more prepared for this than you might think."

There next stop took them to the outskirts of Corvanna, where trades that created bad odours were located. They greeted their Uncle Seth as they passed his tannery but did not stop to chat.

The workshop they entered was signed by a large sheep, cut out of wood, hanging from a metal bar. All Aquila needed to explain was that Sarra needed a traveling cloak, and to part with a gold coin. The tall stout man took Aquila's coin and measured Sarra's height with a tall wooden rule and informed them that it would be delivered the day after next. Being a travelling cloak meant that it would be a generous, full-length, felted cloak with a hood, which would be water resistant, and which could, in emergencies, double up as a blanket, or even as a tent.

Their final call was back near the centre of the town. The back-street shop sported the sign of a quill pen. Inside was a neat shop with a bank of drawers. As Aquila told Scribe Tennon their requirements, he visited the drawers and removed the items to a table, before placing them in a cloth bag for transport and to protect them. They took three quill pens, a small glass stoppered bottle of dark red ink, two more empty stoppered bottles and a stack of parchment sheets. There were more sheets than Sarra felt she would use in a lifetime, but Aquila said they were required, and Mages were profligate with lists and diagrams. Aquila went to pay with a couple of silver coins, but Scribe Tennon said that if she told her father that he needed more supplies of sepia, cuttlefish ink, the commission would be paid.

They thanked him and left to make their way home. They were tired after a long and busy day, and mostly walked in silence, each occupied by their own thoughts.

As they approached their home from the town, along the dusty track, they could see The Swallow drawn up on the beach and their father gutting fish at the edge of the sea, to put on drying racks erected in the sun, between the house and the sea. He had lit a fire near the racks, which, when wet seaweed was added, produced large amounts of smoke. This both flavoured the fish as it dried and kept the flies away. They dropped their baskets at the top of the beach and went to join him. Arron added seaweed to the fire, causing a burst of dark smoke to envelop them, which Arron dismissed with a wave of his hand.

"It must have been a successful trip, if you have excess to dry, Papa." said Sarra, by way of greeting.

"We had a successful trip too." Aquila told him.

"It was very successful, but I am drying the whole catch, except for what we eat fresh, ourselves." answered their father, before going on to explain. "I sailed out on The Great Sea and was hailed by Hallon, who was struggling to take in his nets with the weight of a huge catch of whitefish. He said that the shoal was still there and If I would help him with his nets, we could fill my nets too. So, we fished together, and both brought in a huge catch. I said that I would dry mine so that we didn't take too many to market at the same time and have to drop the price. The shoal was his find, and he will get a good price for his catch now and I will get a good price for dried fish in Winter. Then I raised us a good wind to get us both home while the sun was still high for my smoking and drying them." Arron was pleased that his co-operative venture had benefited himself and Hallon.

"It made an interesting change to be fishing with someone else and not working alone."

Aquila and Sarra both hitched up their skirts and set to work gutting the fish in the shallows. The seabirds feasted on the entrails, and they washed the fish in the sea before passing them to Arron to hang. In that way they were finished quickly, and the flying fish and dogfish caught with the others were set aside for their own dinner.

Aquila cooked the fish while Sarra harvested salads and washed them in the courtyard fountain. Arron sat on the veranda checking his nets, a cup of wine beside him.

"Did Mama make the fountain here as well as the spring, Papa?" Sarra asked, realising how much she had taken it for granted.

"Yes, the day after she and Aquila raised the spring above the back of the garden, she set off for her parent's house. They lived north of Corvenna, near the Highway. She told them about raising the spring for our garden and suggested she could do that for them too. Her parents didn't grow much in their garden but said that a water source next to the house would benefit them greatly, so she caused a spring to rise there, and they had a basin built around it, like ours, only theirs overflowed and ran through a neighbour's garden, who used it for irrigation and ours flows out to the sea. She had to rest then for a whole day, before returning, as the two days' work caused great exhaustion. A tenight later she realised she didn't have to carry water from the garden to the kitchen if she made us a new water source. Her parents commissioned the basin around it to make the fountain."

He peered at his younger daughter. "You haven't suffered any exhaustion, have you, Sarra?"

"I feel as though I have more energy than usual, Papa. I need less sleep too. The only time I felt tired was immediately after using the Mage Map."

"Good, I hope that will continue to be the case."

"The boys will have got to the Mage College today, and if there was someone available, may have spoken to someone about you, but if not, then should do tomorrow. We can, realistically, expect them back in two- or three-days' time, four at the most. They will have had to walk to the Highway before being able to get a cart to the Collage but should be able to get a cart right from the College to Corvanna coming back." Arron put down his nets and took a sip of wine.

"Are you tired, Papa? You travelled a long way and caught a lot of fish over these two days."

"No, not too tired, but I think I shall spend tomorrow with my two daughters while I still have them both here with me. I shall definitely try to take on an apprentice, now though. If Trembil is not interested I will look for someone else. I can teach a boy to sail and fish even if he has no affinity for air."

The two girls looked at each other in surprise, so many things were changing!

7

The following morning the sisters were up not long after dawn. Following breakfast together they made their way to the garden.

It was Sarra's habit on first going to the garden, to take stock of progress and to take mental note of tasks needing to be completed soon, and possible developments for the future. This morning she spoke her thoughts aloud, to pass them on to Aquila.

"The beet are growing well, as are the radish. They will both need plenty of water to swell."

"Should they be watered every day, Sarra? Aquila asked, filling the water jar from the stream.

"Yes, if you can manage it. The sowing stage and the swelling stage are the most critical times for water."

Aquila applied water to the plants and went back for more.

"I can see why the sluice system at Isla Grossa interested you so much."

"These salad leaves and the spicy greens next to them are nearly done. If we pick the rest for the table, we can clear the ground and plant more beans, for winter drying. It isn't good for the soil to keep planting the same crops in one spot. You must try to change things about." Sarra worked as she talked.

Aquila had not realised how knowledgeable her sister was about the plants and their growing needs. She would have to learn as much as possible while Sarra was still at home.

"We will lift the garlic, now and dry it. Its leaves are turning yellow.

We will dry it out under the veranda for a tenight or two, then move it to the store."

"I'm going to leave these few salad plants at the end of the rows. Don't harvest them and they will flower and set seed for collection in one or two moons when they will be dry and ripe, to grow another season, or to gather and sell. Seed collection is an important part of my business."

Sarra instructed and Aquila learned. Aquila felt as if their roles in life had been reversed and felt a new respect for her sister, bordering on awe.

Sarra cleared the ground where the garlic had grown and proposed to grow more salad crops there.

"What shall I do while you sow those?" asked Aquila.

"Why don't you go down to the beach and dig up some razor clams?" was Sarra's suggestion.

"There aren't any razor clams on our beach." protested Aquila.

"There weren't," agreed Sarra. "But I bought a water jar of live ones back from a fishing trip two Summers ago and tipped them into the edge of the sea, and there's a colony of them now. I thought about bringing some mussel encrusted rocks, to seed the rocks at The Point. What do you think?" she asked.

"I think that I've got a very talented and practical sister, who gardens the sea as well as the land!" said Aquila.

Shortly before Sarra was ready to quit the garden for the midday meal, she heard the sound of chatter and laughter heading their way. She looked down the track to see Katerina, Hannish and Hetta, heading her way on a donkey cart. They arrived on the track next to the garden and called across.

"Shall we unload your growing cups here, Sarra, or take them up to the house?" Katerina had her hands full of empty clay growing cups.

"Pass those to me here, please." replied Sarra. "I will have to put soil in them before sowing fresh seeds."

"We brought them to encourage you to come back and grow more." explained Hannah.

"Fester sent me to see what seedlings you had for sale before you sold out. He even volunteered to watch my bread rise, while I came!" Hetta laughed.

After dropping off the clay cups the women drove the cart up to the house and between them, bought all the seedlings growing on the veranda shelves.

"What is your affinity for?" asked Hannish. "Is it earth? That would make sense given how much time you spend with your hands in it, growing things."

"Or is it water, like your mother and your sister? asked Katerina.

Sarra's gaze switched between the three questioning faces.

"You wouldn't believe how quickly she can turn water to ice!" Aquila cut in, relieving the situation.

Having loaded up the cart and filling Sarra's hands with copper and a few silver coin, they wished Sarra well at Mage College and went on their way back to town. Sarra piled the coins next to her father's cup.

"Towards the cost, Papa." she said.

"That is all taken care of." insisted Arron. "But I will take this to the money-changer and get it all changed into silver, so that it's easier for you to store or carry."

After the midday meal Arron told the girls that he was heading into Corvanna, to the moneychanger, the brewer and a few other errands.

Having worked hard in the garden all morning, the girls decided to rest in the heat of the afternoon.

Sarra was wakened by the sound of another donkey cart approaching. She slipped her dress back on and moved out to see who was there.

The donkey cart pulled up in a cloud of dust. There had rarely been so much use of the track, it led nowhere else, but only continued as a footpath to The Point.

"Good afternoon, Mistress Sarra." said Janus.

Was it what he said, or the way that he said it, that made her skin cold and clammy?

"Good afternoon, Farmer Janus" Sarra replied politely.

"Is your father at home, today?" Janus asked.

"I'm afraid you have been unlucky again. He had some business to conduct in Corvanna." stated Sarra.

"He seems to be away from home, much, recently." complained Janus.

"It is the fate of a busy man, I suppose." replied Sarra.

"I came on another matter too. I hear you are selling up your stock of seedlings." Janus went on.

"Indeed?" questioned Sarra.

"I came to look at them. As a farmer with a reputation to uphold, I would not want to be associated with anyone who grew inferior plant stock."

"Indeed! Neither would I." snapped back Sarra. "I have a fine reputation, and would not wish to harm it, but since I have regular customers coming to my door for my seedlings, I think that is not likely! In fact, there are no seedlings for you to look at. All of my seedling plants were sold this morning to collecting customers."

"It is good to know that you have a fine reputation, even if that comes from your own mouth. It is a shame, too, that I cannot see for myself." Janus sounded less than convinced. Almost everything he said seemed to rile Sarra.

"I will ask around the town about your seedlings before I ask your father about walking out with you. I would wish to be certain." Jason's cheeks were flushed with frustration.

"You should not bother yourself, as I may be called away to Mage Collage soon." she informed him.

"Well so MAY we all! Some of us live real lives, in a real world, and don't wait for MAYBES, to possibly come along, then wake up and find out that real possibilities of advancement have passed us by!" said Janus crossly.

"I will tell my father you came. Shall I tell him you wished to discuss building a windmill?" Sarra asked.

"I may look elsewhere." Janus said dismissively.

"Goodbye Janus." Sarra muttered as Janus moved his donkey on, to turn his cart around.

When Arron returned the sun was nearing the horizon. He carried with him a jar of wine. There were cold dishes to pick at, on the table.

"Try this, girls. It is very good. There will be more delivered tomorrow, and ale too, my stores were much depleted by our celebration." He poured some into three cups. "Your Aunt Kiera will be coming by in the morning too."

"It is always good to see her." Sarra was glad that she was coming. Chatting to her would keep her busy and prevent her dwelling on whether she would be wanted by Mage College and what she would find there if she was. Though it would be difficult to avoid her awkward questions, Aquila would help her with that.

"Janus was here again today, Papa." Sarra said. Then dismissed him from her mind.

Aquila told her father about all they had achieved in the garden that morning. It seemed strange to hear his elder daughter enthusing about plants, but he was heartened by the new respect he heard in her voice when she talked of the things Sarra had taught her.

8

They had finished breakfast, attended to the chickens and goat, but not yet decided what to do with the day, when they heard voices approaching, accompanied by the sound of cartwheels.

Aunt Kiera appeared in the courtyard first, followed by cousins Guyor and Trembil, her eldest children, and twins.

"We had just set off when Cobbler Fendi offered us a ride in his cart. He has a parcel from Felter Crom, for you too. Such a busy time!"

The cobbler appeared around the corner of the house, carrying a wrapped parcel and a basket. He joined them, sitting on the stone bench and setting his basket on the table. From the basket he first produced a pair of stout black boots which he insisted Sarra try on immediately. She removed her worn sandals, which Fendi tutted over, and put on the boots. Fendi prodded at the boots to feel her feet through the thick leather. When he was satisfied that her toes had enough room, he had her walk up and down to demonstrate their fit. He then had her take these off and put on the new sandals. This time there was no prodding as he could see her toes, but he had her wiggling them, before walking up and down the courtyard again. Finally, the slippers had to be tested, and as well as walking, he had her skipping up and dawn and dancing in circles. Finally satisfied, he handed Arron the parcel from Felter Crom.

Arron had poured Cobbler Fendi a cup of wine and he now allowed himself a drink, satisfied with the fit of his fashioning.

"It is an expensive time, to equip a child for Mage College." He commented.

Sarra felt herself go hot at the thought that she might not be invited,

73

and these people would all know of her expectations and subsequent shame.

"It is." her father agreed. "But her training will pay for itself, and they will pay most of my and her expenses while she is there. When she is trained, she will be set up to do anything she wants. It is a good thing to have a child go to Mage College, and I should know, she will be my third!"

Sarra carefully unwrapped the parcel, since it was wrapped in a large piece of felt and tied with a leather throng, both of which would be reused. She unfolded and put on the dark blue travelling cloak. She put up the voluminous hood, which almost hid her face, then holding the two front edges together, she swept round the courtyard modelling the garment.

The cobbler chuckled, Arron roared with laughter and her aunt and cousins clapped and whistled.

"I SEE YOU ARE READY TO GO, THEN?!" The stranger's voice cut through their laughter like a honed sword.

Sarra stopped dead in her tracks and Aquila dropped the cup she was holding, to shatter on the stone tiles of the courtyard.

"Mage Ichor!" Aquila turned and dropped a deep curtsey.

"Aquila, my dear, so good of you to remember. Perhaps you could do the introductions?"

"Certainly, Sir." She gestured: "This is my Father, Master Fisher and Affine Arron; this is Master Cobbler Fendi, who has delivered boots, sandals and slippers to my sister today; this is my sister, Sarra, who you will have heard about from my brother, Fern; and these are my Aunt Kiera who has delivered my sister's new clothing; and my cousins Guyor and Trembil who will undertake some of my sister's duties if she is invited to Mage College." Aquila ended her litany of introductions.

"IF?" Mage Ichor roared. "IF? Either your brother has lied about her abilities, or you have taken leave of your senses! There is no IF! I have come to settle the necessary arrangements and conduct her there myself!"

"Now, Affine Aquila, is there another cup for that wine, or have you broken them all? It has been a long and tedious journey."

Fern and Sten had appeared around the corner of the house and taken a seat during Mage Ichor's introductions. They now collected cups and took then to Aquila to be filled too. The company set chatting about irrelevancies and drinking water and wine for some time.

Aquila suggested to Trembil that he helped her look for crabs and shellfish at The Point, and they moved off down the path.

Brewer Festor arrived in the courtyard, announcing that he had wine and ale in his cart, but couldn't get near to the house for the other two donkey carts.

"You'll have to devise a parking area if you regularly get so many visitors, Master Fisherman Arron." he advised.

"Affine Arron may well have to think about that." agreed Mage Ichor, with the emphasis on 'Affine'.

"I have lingered too long, and should go, now that I know Sarra's shoes are a good fit." said Cobbler Fendi. "My cart is blocking the way." He took his leave.

Fern and Sten went with Brewer Festor to help unload the wine and even Mage Ichor lent a hand. Brewer Festor had brought a small flask of wine that Arron had not ordered, as a sample, and Arron, Festor and Mage Ichor walked down the beach, then sat on the bows of The Swallow and discussed its merits.

Aunt Kera encouraged Sarra to show Guyor her garden and suggested they could gather vegetables for dinner.

By the time dinner was laid out on the courtyard table, Mage Ichor had a quill and parchment to hand to take notes, and Arron had provided a small dish of cuttlefish ink.

"So Sarra, if I am to make recompense for your being away from your duties, I need to know how you normally spend your day."

Mage Ichor's tone was kind enough, but he still made her nervous, particularly with quill poised, waiting for her to speak.

Sarra took a deep breath and began: "After I have risen, I lay breakfast out. After we have breakfasted, I first milk the goat and make ready the next day's yoghurt; I feed the chickens and collect the eggs; I carry water in the garden to the crops and drench them before it gets too warm and they wilt, and I give water to the seedling pots on the veranda shelves. What I do next depends on whether it is a market day or not: If it is, might pick produce in a basket, or load seedlings into one, or pack fish into a carry-basket and walk to market early to sell my or my father's wares; If it is not a market day I will weed and hoe in the garden; I may clear ground and sow new seeds; I may fill and sew new seeds in growing cups, if there is room on the shelves, for replanting in the garden when they are grown or taking to market; I will pick salads and vegetables for both daily meals; on some days I will wash our clothes and hang them to dry in the breeze to dry; on other days I will clean the house; some days I might accompany my father in collecting shellfish or fishing for crabs or gutting fish; depending on the season: there will be the bees to tend; or honey to take; or jams and chutneys to make; or beans to shell and dry; or grapes to be put on racks to dry; and these dried foods must all be put in clay or glass jars and stored. Every day there are two meals to prepare for whoever is in the house, sometimes just me, or sometimes the four of us plus a guest or two; sometimes there is shopping to be done or commissions to make or errands to run for father in Corvanna, but I usually combine those with going to market to save time. Apart from that my time is my own, to visit friends or relations, to walk the coast, to sew, to read in the library in Corvanna, to increase my learning, or whatever I want."

"Quite the lady of leisure, then." said the Mage, ruefully. "I can see why it would take two of your cousins to cover your tasks!"

"Oh, no sir. They are both at the end of their schooling now and will be moving into work, but each into a different type of work. Guyor will take on my house and garden tasks for part of her time, they are things which will help her learn to be a good wife, but also, she will be learning weaving at her mother's loom, Aunt Kiera is the best linen weaver in the area. Trembil will take on my tasks with father, running errands, helping with the light fishing, gutting, drying and taking the catch to market. If they turn out to be a good fit, he will apprentice to father as a fisherman, as he does not want to follow his father's trade in tanning.

"Guyor and Trembil are happy with this arrangement?" Questioned Mage Ichor.

"Oh, yes. It gives Trembil the chance to try out a trade before committing himself to a full apprenticeship, and meanwhile he will have earnings to buy tools for a different trade, if it does not take. Guyor is planning to use her earnings to commission Carpenter Daffid to build her a loom of her own. It will really help set her up."

Sarra looked across to her cousins who had been listening and who nodded in agreement.

"Then to practicalities – will your cousins need lodgings near here? – not that there seems to be anywhere near here!"

Arron answered that point. "No, Trembil will live here. We fishermen do not keep scribe's hours. Guyor will live at home, also working with her mother on the weaving. I have a donkey and cart arriving tomorrow which will also be for her to use to travel to and from Corvanna."

"The donkey and cart should be here in the morning along with beams and tiles for the building of a stable and cart store and adding some more rooms to my home." Arron sat back, looking very pleased with himself.

"Donkey and cart, stable, cart store and extra rooms." muttered Mage Ichor, making notes. "This has entailed quite some outlay for you."

"I am a successful fisherman and have earnings from my Affinity with air. We have lived well within our means for many years. I have savings." responded Arron.

"Nevertheless, there will be some recompense for you, in addition to the wages of your niece and nephew. Sarra's outfitting must also be covered by the College. She needs four extra complete sets of clothes as she will not have time to launder clothes, as well as walking boots, indoor slippers and outdoor sandals; personal effects and stationery. I have already seen her travelling cloak; how does she do on the rest?"

Aunt Kiera answered the clothing question. "Most of the weavings for her clothes are done and she has had most. I have one dress to complete and her underthings to put together, it shouldn't take more than two days at the most, including the back sack to carry them in, when she needs to travel."

The Mage nodded his approval and turned his attention back to Sarra. "Can you appraise your cousins of their tasks in two days? Show them what must be done for them to take your place?" he raised an eyebrow and his quill waiting for her response.

"I can show Guyor what will need doing in the garden and introduce her to the goat and the chickens." said Sarra. "And Aquila will be here to show her around the house, even after I have left. I can show her where I keep the drying racks and storage jars that she may need before I return. I will be able to show Trembil where the fish racks and carrying nets and baskets are and where to find clams and prawns and crabs, but the rest will be for father to show him. I can be ready."

The Mage looked pleased, as far as they were able to tell.

"And for myself, will I be able to find two night's lodgings, hereabouts?" he asked.

"The nearest lodging house to here is in Torroja, at least half a day's travel away." Arron replied. "We have already talked about this" nodding at the two young men. "Sten and Fern will take my room, as I have a married man's mattress, and I will sleep in Fern's room, which will free up our guest room again, for you."

"Then we shall have a busy two days before our departure" said the Mage, to all the diners. Then to Arron: "We will begin in the morning with a visit to the money-changer in Corvanna so that I can get coin for all your immediate expenses and the first six tenights wages for Guyor and Trembil. Sarra will be gone at least that time. Her training will be covered by earnings from commissions undertaken in training her. Where she goes and what she does after training will be up to her, of course, though we hope that she will fully utilise her training. Many opportunities will present themselves that no-one can, as yet, foresee."

Sarra put her arm round Arron's waist to hold him close. "I will come home, Papa."

"Only if it is what you want, Sarra. It is as Mage Ichor says, you do not know what opportunities will present themselves."

The Mage suggested that Aunt Kiera and her children should take his donkey and cart and that the children could return in it, in the morning.

Sarra and Aquilla cleared up and made for bed, leaving Arron and Mage Ichor to broach a new jar of wine, Arron and Sten to discuss the terms of Arron's commission for building works, and all of them to sort out the sleeping arrangements.

Unsurprisingly, Sarra and Aquila had breakfasted and Guyor and Trembil arrived before the four men joined them at the courtyard table to break their fast.

Arron and the Mage were soon ready to leave for Corvanna in the Mage's returned cart. Sten and Fern commandeered Arron's newly arrived cart for acquiring lime rock, the basis, with sand, which could be taken from the beach, for making mortar for the building work.

Sarra told her brother "We'll have to introduce the donkey to Hella, later. They've no choice but to get on, anyway, as there is only one piece of fenced off land for animals. I think I'll call him Vessas, as he reminds me of Wessas."

"Not as stubborn and a faster leaner, I hope!" joked Fern.

Aquila suggested that she took Trembil to show him where to find crabs, prawns and clams for a fish stew for dinner and leave Guyor and Sarra to garden chores.

Guyor's small fingers quickly took to milking, and Hetta was completely co-operative. After feeding the chickens and collecting eggs, Sarra took Guyor to the kitchen, to show her how to mix some of the milk in with the remainder of the yogurt and set it aside to produce more yoghurt. She told Guyor that the kid should be ready for Arron or Trembil to take to slaughter in about two moons, but if she were not back, to remind Arron. They chatted and worked together in the garden, gathering salads to go with the eggs for lunch and vegetables to add to the fish stew, before returning to the courtyard fountain to wash these. Sarra showed Guyor how to divert water to the indoor kitchen when it was needed, then introduced her to her store cupboard of preserved foods and eastern spices, which she advised her to use sparingly. She showed Guyor where she brought seedlings on, on the shelves under the protection of the veranda. As they sat having a cooling drink, Guyor shared her thoughts with Sarra.

"Hella always produces plenty of milk, so when there are few people living here, there must be an excess?" asked Guyor.

"Yes. I had thought that if I got a pig to rear, that would take up any excesses, but I have done nothing about it yet"

"I have a friend whose mother makes cheese. I will ask her how it is done. "I could practice on any excess milk and acquire another skill." said Guyor with satisfaction.

"You will be learning many new skills, as it is, are they not enough?" questioned Sarra.

"They are all skills that will make me a better bride prospect or that I could use in a marriage, to earn coin. I will be more attractive as a potential bride when I leave here, and more so again when I have my own loom."

Sarra was staggered by Guyor's disclosures. "I have never really thought along those lines." confessed Sarra.

"You don't need to plan your future out so carefully, now you are going to Mage College." pointed out Guyor.

"No, but perhaps they are things I should have thought about before!" Sarra was contrite.

"You were always a good catch, as a bride, though! You grew all the food here, except for the fish, and earned coin from taking your seeds, seedlings and produce to market. Even Janus seemed interested in you." Guyor confided.

"That I can do without!" sighed Sarra.

"You can't have too many prospects, or admirers, or skills, and yours certainly aren't getting any less." summed up Guyor.

This didn't cheer Sarra any, but she couldn't help but admire her cousin for her long-term planning. Her own future seemed very uncertain at this moment, but then, she had never had a long-term strategy, anyway.

"I have so much to learn from you, before you go…" Guyor stood and moved back towards the garden.

"I think there's an awful lot I could learn from you." said Sarra, following.

Sarra set Guyor to filling the growing cups and planting seeds in them.

"All of them look alike, until they are grown, so it's particularly important that they are labelled. I write on the slate label with a piece of chalk rock, its type and a number, when I am planting lots, that tells me which are oldest. Today will be 143, as I've planted on 142 days up to now, this season." Sarra instructed. The two girls worked in harmony, filling, planting labelling, then stacking the cups in a deep basket to carry to the courtyard.

Arron and the Mage were the first to return. Sarra and Guyor went to unhitch the donkey and led him up to the field to meet the goats.

"This is Vessus." said Sarra to the goats. "Vessus, be nice to Hella and her kid. He won't be here long, but Hella is always here, and though they are smaller that you are, they both have horns." Vessus and Hella touched noses, though the kid just frisked about. Then they all got on with the important task of grazing.

Returning to the courtyard, they found Arron looking at the shelves, newly filled with rows of planting cups. "You have both been very busy." he said.

"We had two pairs of hands working, and Guyor learns very quickly. Having sold all my stock, there was lots of space to fill. There will also be extra mouths to feed, Papa, even without me, with Aquila, Fern, Sten and Trembil staying here, and Guyor too some of the time."

The Mage had taken up his customary position at the table, quill in hand and a sheaf of parchment in front of him. He ignored the lunch platters of food being set on the table around him as he sketched out plans, verbalising as he sketched.

"You have, at the moment, as well as one indoor living/kitchen area and store; five bedrooms: for yourself; your three children and a guest room currently occupied by Sten, or me, for these few days; but five bedrooms nevertheless, all full; a courtyard with outdoor kitchen and a fountain; a stone table and benches, and a superb view!"

"If you assume that Sarra returns here after Mage College, with yourself, Aquila and Fern as three of her four Elementals, you will still need bedrooms for you three, for Sarra and the fourth Elemental (Sten or not); a guest room or two; storage for your donkey cart, which can store other things too; a designated study/workroom for your Mage, and a room for your housekeeper/cook, as none of you will have time to give to that role." The more the Mage talked and added to his list, the nor complex things became, and the larger the house needed to grow.

"That assumes that Sarra works with only four Elementals, of course. These days most Mages work with eight, and some with twelve Elementals. There is no shortage of candidates for Elementals, or commissions to take, but there is great shortage of Mages."

Arron took over the conversation: "Let us assume, for now, that Sarra returns, and her four Elementals are myself, Aquila, Fern and Sten, or any other Earth Affine, that I have apprentice Trembil, and that the indoor area doubles as a study/workroom. With the guestroom, it means increasing the house by two bedrooms and a cart room. That would at least take care of a beginning, and we could expand later if we needed to."

Mage Ichor tried to put his points again, while struggling to stay reasonable.

"If you are Sarra's Air Elemental you are unlikely to have much time for fishing, let alone training an apprentice, but that would free his room for the cook/housekeeper. No Mage has time to cook food, let alone grow it. You WILL need a room as a separate workroom/study for the Mage and MORE THAN ONE guest room as people will flock to a new Mage with commissions. A minimum or four extra rooms and a cart room will be needed." The Mage took a deep calming breath and continued.

"This would be best achieved by extending the two wings of your house by two rooms each, along with the veranda and consequently giving you a larger courtyard between, with room for another stone table and benches, all with a view! The Mage College will pay for half of the costs, IF and only if, Sarra returns here as a working Mage."

This new aspect concerned Sarra greatly and so she interrupted the discussion.

"Papa, I will return home, but I know that you may not want to become my Air Elemental, as it would mean so many changes in your life. I don't want you to commit coin and effort into expanding the house because of me."

Aaron tried to quell her fears: "Sten will give me a good rate on the building commission in return for having lodgings here, if he charges me at all, and Fern will do it free, as they are both anxious to enable you to come back and work here as a Mage, preferably with them as Elementals. You have enabled me to run a very frugal household, so I have savings. I also have the promise of help obtaining stone for the building, as you will see tomorrow. This house has grown too small for the four of us, five with Sten, anyway. Taking Trembil as apprentice and buying a donkey and cart, which I should have done long ago, to help with getting to the market, means that it really needs to be done now."

He summed up: "Mage Ichor is right. A Master Fisher with an apprentice and three children with affinities needs a large house, anyway, let alone having a Mage as a daughter. We will build on four extra rooms and a cart store and expand the courtyard.

Arron turned to the Mage. "Scratch out your plans, Mage Ichor, for I have friends coming with boats tomorrow, and I need to know how much reef rock I need."

Fern and Sten, Aquila and Trembil couldn't have timed their arrival, back at the table, better.

"Yes." Agreed Sarra. "But after lunch. No-one works well on an empty stomach."

Aquila and Trembil took their baskets of shellfish to the indoor kitchen and washed their hands in the fountain before sitting down.

"A successful trip?" Aquila asked her brother.

Fern beamed. "Yes very! Although we may have rather more lime rock than we need, but we don't have to use it all at once, we can pile some up out of the way, and store it. We got it all in exchange for our expert services at the quarry."

"I think you'll find that there isn't too much lime rock for what the Mage has in mind." Said Arron ruefully. "I am going to need to order more oak beams and floor and roof tiles and more stone for the courtyard. I'm not sure how to tell my friends tomorrow that we'll need double, or even treble, the quantity of reef rock."

"Yes, I was thinking about that." said Sten. "If Sarra lends me a hand tomorrow to 'lighten the load' things should go a lot quicker and easier, particularly if we need more stone."

"Excellent idea, Sten." Mage Ichor became the centre of attention again. "I will lend a hand. It would be a good thing if I worked with Sarra in this respect, too, and we experience working together. It will be well worthwhile, even if it holds us up for an extra day."

Sarra was baffled. "If it saves time, then why would it hold us up for an extra day?"

Everyone waited for his answer.

"Because I did not know we were going to move stone tomorrow and had meant to ask Arron if he would convey us to the Isla Grossa to make an assessment of the Mage Tower that you visited, and it's map room. I can't really return to Mage College, having come all this way, before I have seen it for myself. Would it be alright with everyone if we visited there the day after tomorrow, before Sarra and I departed the following day?"

Everyone waited for someone else to reply. Eventually Sarra took the initiative. "I think that would be an excellent plan. I really would like the opportunity to go back, myself, and have another look round. We did leave in rather a hurry, and without two blankets and three carry nets too."

"Can I go too?" begged an excited Trembil.

"I don't think Swallow would hold everyone." answered Arron.

"Affines only." stated the Mage, emphatically.

Sarra tried to soften the blow. "I think it might be a good idea for you to go home and pack your things, then you can take over my room, while I'm gone, before your new room gets built."

Trembil decided he could make do with that! He also had not had chance to tell his friends that he had got an apprenticeship, yet, or that his cousin was going to Mage College. He had lots of news to spread!

Lunch lasted longer than usual as there was much to be discussed. They were still seated around the table when Janus swaggered around the corner of the house, into the courtyard. Although he had not expected to encounter such a crowd of people, he puffed up his chest and addressed Arron in a loud voice.

"I had expected you to call on me, at my house, this morning! I trust your younger daughter was not too busy or too empty-headed to not relay my message to you? I wished to discuss a possible commission for a windmill on my property, which I will want to complete as soon as possible! I also want you to tell your daughter that she may start walking out with me, with a possible view to marriage, if I find her agreeable."

Sarra's blood drained from her face, she felt cold and sick. Others in the group also felt sick, but hot and angry. Arron froze in horror at his words, and was about to rise and lambast him, but was beaten to this by the Mage.

Mage Ichor rose to his feet and took a deep breath. He used the voice he addressed vast numbers of Affines with: "I don't know who you are, you excuse of a man, but Affine Arron is far too busy to deal with the likes of you, or to take your measly commission. There are matters of great importance being discussed here and we do not take kindly to your rude interruption! The 'empty-headed' daughter that you, apparently, and most inappropriately, had designs on making your wife, has a much greater destiny to fulfil, after her training, with me, at Mage College."

Janus shrank visibly and took a small step back. He addressed his next remarks at Sarra. "So, you really are going to Mage College? You think you have an affinity? I wouldn't object to my wife being an Affine."

Sarra was saved from replying by the Mage.

"ARE YOU STILL HERE? Have you no idea of the status of these people? This girl is as far above you as a peacock is an ant! Sarra does not have an affinity with an element, she has an affinity with all four elements, she has an affinity with the essence of life itself! She will be enrolling at Mage College in three days' time, and when she returns, she will not BE an AFFINE, she will be a FULLY TRAINED, WORKING MAGE!"

Janus backed rapidly a couple of steps, tripped, and then turned and fled.

Somehow the Mage's outburst and the certainties he had expressed gave Sarra great confidence in herself and in her future. All her doubts had been swept away in those few moments.

The afternoon passed mostly in making plans and, where appropriate, lists and diagrams. Sarra and Guyor cooked diner, a fish stew enhanced with smoked ground peppers and saffron. It was to be followed by a desert cooked by Gaynor, of eggs, milk, honey and nutmeg, baked in a warm oven, and fresh strawberries. The Mage was impressed by the seafood stew, to which Sarra had added dried whitefish.

"I must say, Sarra, I had not expected you to be such a learned cook or to be seeing you using exotic spices from the East. Fern sang your praises in many respects but failed to mention that." he said.

"We have a travelling spice seller who calls at our market occasionally and encourages me to spend the coppers I have earned selling seedlings." she confessed. "I enjoy trying his wares and have built up a collection."

"But you use them with great discretion." added the Mage. "It is good to see discretion in an up-and-coming Mage. We are, essentially, a brash and forceful breed. It is probably that that led to what we call the Mage Wars.

As soon as dinner was over, Guyor and Trembil left for home on Arron's donkey cart. Sten insisted that he needed everyone fit and strong for the morning's work and enforced an early night.

9

Sarra woke just before dawn and, knowing what a busy day it would be, washed and dressed immediately before sleep could claim her again. She had milked the goat and tended the chickens before anyone else was up. Then, putting breakfast ready, she went to water the garden, knowing that there would be no time later.

When she returned to the courtyard, she was greeted first by Fern. "Sarra, you need to eat! You will need all your strength today. Sit and eat and we will make plans."

Fern and Sten often worked together on building commissions, as Sten worked with the stone, and Fern could heat up the lime rock to high temperatures as part of making the mortar to bind them. They and the Mage were pouring over the sketches he had made the previous day.

"We will need a vast amount of stone." Sten told Arron. "Where were you planning on getting it all from?"

"I built this house from reef rock, as most of the buildings around here are. We don't take it from the reef itself as that might weaken the protection given to the lagoon from the storms on The Great Sea. We take it from three or four of the uninhabited islands and bring it here by boat. I've got many friends coming today, with their boats to help us."

"It will take many boatloads to match up to Mage Ichor's plans. It may be necessary to get what we can today and start building, and then go and get another supply later." Fern sounded rather despondent.

"We need to get as much as possible while Sarra is here, to help me." Sten insisted.

"Then we had better start now." said Arron rising from his seat. He had been facing the lagoon and had seen his friend's boats approaching. "Fern, you bring Swallow, with the others. Sarra and I will go with Guss, then we can tell everyone our plans on the way."

"Aquila, can you take the cart to Corvanna and pick up a cask of ale and some wine jars I've ordered from Brewer Festor? Your Aunt Kiera will come back with Guyor bringing the orders from Baker Hetta for rolls and pies, with her, so it will be up to the three of you to prepare lunch for when we return with the stone."

Arron took Sarra's hand and hurried her to the shore to meet Guss' boat, then swept Sarra up in his arms and waded out to The Sea Urchin and swung Sarra on board.

"Wait for me!" shouted Sten, running after them and wading out to haul himself aboard just after Arron.

"To the Isle of Stone!" Arron yelled to the other boats, which tacked about and started heading out again. Behind them, Fern pushed Swallow into the shallows, climbed aboard and raised the sail. Mage Ichor approached more slowly, but once aboard directed Fern to the tiller, saying that he would widen the range of Arron's following wind.

As the flotilla of fishing boats made their way across the lagoon, Sten explained his plan to Sarra. "We need to find large pieces of stone, but small enough for a man to get his arms around."

"But they'll be too heavy to lift!" objected Sarra.

"Not once we've 'persuaded' them to leave most of their weight on the island."

Sarra was astonished and bemused. "But won't that make them too weak to build a house?"

Sten didn't mind imparting trade secrets to someone who would soon be learning them, and a whole lot more besides. "Once I've mortared them together into a wall, they will discover a great desire to be heavy again, and gain weight from the ground, and as that is linked to the island, nothing is gained or lost, just moved temporarily."

There was a problem, however, as the following wind Arron had raised enabled the other boats to reach the island before they did. The fishermen had beached their boats and were filling them with watermelon sized pieces of stone, which they had struggled to lift, and even now the boats were sitting lower in the water.

"NO" Yelled Sten. "STOP. You are giving the boats too heavy a load. Wait for me! Only load the rocks I tell you."

The fishermen stopped but didn't look convinced. Sten looked pointedly at Arron.

"He's right." confirmed Arron. "He's the expert. Let him show you which rocks to load."

Sten stepped from boat to boat, using them like steppingstones, to reach the shore. "Sarra, I need your help. Please lend me your strength."

Sarra followed Sten's path, but it took her longer to get ashore.

"This one." said Sten referring to a large boulder under his right hand, his left hand clasping Sarra's.

"Caylon, you'll need to give me a hand with this!" said Hallon, looking at the rock.

"You'll be surprised." said Sten. They both were, when, picking it up together, they nearly threw it instead of lifting it!

"Right." said Hallon, to Sten, "You choose the light ones, and we'll pack them in the boats."

Soon the four original boats that had begun loading early were low in the water and ready set off for Arron's home.

"Can't you make the first stones they put in, lighter?" asked Sarra.

"No, they aren't touching the ground, so there's nowhere for the weight to go." explained Sten.

Arron suggested those boats head for home. "But don't drink all the Ale!" he shouted after them.

"And put the heavy and light rocks in different piles!" Sten added.

When Sarra held on to Sten's hand, opening her mind to him, she could sense the stones as he did, losing their weight into the ground below. This made things quicker and less tiring for Sten, and soon they had used all of the suitable sized boulders and some of those he thought of as being rather small. The three other loaded boats set off for home too, leaving Arron's Swallow and Hallon's Bowline empty and waiting. The boats' journey back, without a magically raised following wind would take much longer and involve much manoeuvring of sails and tacking.

"What about the other side of the island?" asked Mage Ichor.

"A sheer cliff, with deep water below. There's no stone for building there." answered Hallon.

Arron and Hallon began to discuss the stone on nearby islands.

"Let me search." said the Mage, before he clambered up the steep incline at a speed that belied his age and size.

Sarra, Sten, Arron, Fern and Hallon sat down, preparing for a long wait, but hadn't been waiting too long when a shout was heard from the ridge.

"I've found something." shouted the Mage. "Sten, Sarra, I need you both. Can you climb up here?"

Sten began to make his way up, then turned back to give Sarra a hand. Sarra, greatly regretting wearing a dress and not trews and tunic, hitched her dress to knee length, and took Sten's offer of help. They made good time to the top of the ridge, where they found the island opened, and become a plateau.

"This island has a strange rock formation." Mage Ichor told them. "With the strata running East to West across the island, in a vertical plane."

Sarra looked at Sten, who didn't look as bemused as she felt.

"Near the Northern cliff there is a cleft, where a fault has not entirely split away, but is very weak." the Mage continued. "It narrows at the Eastern end and gets closer to the cliff there too. That is where I want to work on it." he pointed East, and they made their way over the plateau.

"You think we can split it away completely? asked Sten.

"I'm certain we could do that. That isn't the problem." the Mage addressed his remarks to Sten. "If we split that section of rock away it will collapse into the sea and sink to the depths, never to be seen again."

The Mage made sure he had Sten's full attention. "You recall that underwater fire-mountains can produce rock that had air bubbles in it, that is lighter than water, so that it floats? We need to make the rock that light before we split it away. It will not be easy; you know the effort it takes to lighten rock at all. I wouldn't normally try to make rock that light." the Mage explained it all, taking his cue from Sten's nods.

The three had walked as they talked, and now approached the top of a sheer cliff. An arm's length in front of the cliff was a cleft which seemed to drop into the bowels of the earth. Sarra took Sten's hand as they got closer. Mage Ichor stood close at the edge of the cleft, with perfect calm and confidence. He gestured to the East and the three walked that way, together. The cleft narrowed as they walked along and got closer to the cliff edge. Eventually they reached a spot where the cleft was only a hand's span wide and only a hands length from the cliff edge.

"We work here." announced the Mage. He lay down and reached across the cleft to lay his hands on the rock on the other side of the gap.

"Lie down either side of me with your hands on the far rock and your fingers touching mine." he ordered.

Sarra had got used to 'feeling' the rock with Sten from her work with him at the shore, so she opened her mind and gasped at the strength of rapport they had with the rock. The slab of rock was breaking away from the main section of rock. It was peeling away, crack by crack, slowly it was separating. She felt the Mage 'telling' the rock that it would be easier to part if it was lighter. Sarra felt the Mage and Sten force the weight down into the earth, down, down, far below the seabed, the weight kept sinking. The rock felt light, so exceptionally light, Sarra felt almost dizzy with the lightness. It became harder to think, harder to separate herself from the rock. She was high up above the sea, she was going to fall from the cliff into the sea. No – it was not her; it was the rock. Sarra felt lightheaded and dizzy, experiencing a moment of vertigo, she had spots in front of her eyes.

There was a sudden crack, a sound like thunder and the rock under their hands fell away, leaving their hands dangling over the edge of the cliff.

The thin slice of rock shattered as it fell, crashing into the sea as large pieces, which broke up further, on impact with the water, sending up plumes of foam.

The three rose to their feet, and. peering over the cliff. saw chunks of rock bob to the surface and form a raft of floating debris. The rock raft took on the shape of the water, with undulating waves running across it. Slowly, almost imperceptibly, it began to drift away from the cliff.

"Quick!" said the Mage setting off. "Quick. We need to get back to the others!" They started to run across the plateau towards the South side of the island. When they started down the slope Arron, Fern and Hallon were shouting questions at them.

"What happened?"

"Are you alright?"

"What was that noise?"

"Is something happening?"

"Is anyone injured?"

They didn't answer as they needed all their breath for the scramble down to the shore.

"Into the boats." gasped Sten.

The mage just held his sides and pointed.

Sten went straight to Hallon's boat, but pushed it into the shallows, before clambering in, himself. Hallon pushed away from the shore with an oar and raised the sail. Arron helped the Mage and Sarra aboard before pushing off, then leapt aboard as Fern raised the sail.

"The other side of the island." Sten shouted over to Arron, taking hold of Bowline's tiller.

Beside the seat Sten was sitting on was a box of fishing nets. Sten picked up a net with the hand not occupied with the tiller. There was a row of cork floats along one edge.

"How long is this net, Hallon?"

"About half a league." answered Hallon. "I meant to take them out, to make more room, but all of the others were already leaving, and I didn't want to be left behind."

"That's great, Hallon." said a relieved Sten. "Can we get close enough to Arron to talk? Well shout, anyway?"

They were still working their way round the island.

"Of course." Hallon adjusted his sail slightly and the boats slowly grew closer.

"Hallon has a net." Sten shouted over to Arron. "When we get there, we can fasten it between the two boats." Sten assumed that Sarra and the Mage had told him of developments.

Hallon looked confused. "We are fishing?" he asked incredulously.

As they rounded the island the floating raft of rock came into view. It had dispersed slightly, but mostly still floated as a mass, distorted by waves, drifting very slowly away from the island.

"What is that?" asked Hallon.

"Rock." Sten replied.

"It's floating!" stated Hallon.

"It's very light rock!" Sten replied.

Hallon said nothing, but just shook his head.

Arron manovered his boat closer. Sten tied one end of a rope to the net and threw the other end of the rope to Arron. At a signal from Arron, Hallon dropped his anchor overboard. Arron pulled in the rope as Sten let the net out, then tied it off to the Swallow. He manovered Swallow between the rock and the island, Sten paying out the net as he went.

"Take up the anchor." said Sten, who could see he was nearing the end of the net. He fixed the end of the net to Bowline.

"Sail slowly away from the island, in line with Arron." requested Sten.

As the two boats headed gently away from the island, the net formed a loop around the raft of rock and towed it gently Northwards. Very steadily Arron came around to a westerly heading, Hallon mirroring his actions, and then to a southerly direction. Keeping both boats sailing in the same direction at the same speed was a straightforward task for an Air Affine of Arron's ability, even without the Mage's help.

When they reached Arron's home, the previous loads had been stacked in two areas of the upper beach. On seeing the sight of the boats towing something in a net the men finished the ale in their cups and set their cups down, to move to the water's edge.

The task of stacking the ultra-light rock in a third area was achieved quickly and with a certain amount of raucous revelry, the men forming chains to toss the rocks from man to man!

As soon as the task was done, Arron thanked everyone for their help: "My good friends, it has been quite a day This huge feat of rock gathering has been made easier, more exciting, and a unique experience by our good friends Mage Ichor, Affine Sten and my daughter Sarra. But it would not have been possible at all without all of you, my life-long friends and fellow fishermen, the fleet of Corvanna! Now, take up your cups again, fill them with ale, eat and drink with me and celebrate Sarra's imminent departure to the Mage College."

Aunt Kiera had forced her way through the line of fishermen who had been moving rock, to reach Sarra, sitting on the side of Swallow, watching the activity with Fern and Sten.

"SARRA, have you no shame!" Kiera was red in the face, eyes shining brightly.

"Aunt?" Sarra was both distressed and puzzled by her aunt's outburst.

"YOUR DRESS! Your knees!" the first two words were shouted, the second two whispered. She did not want to draw everyone's attention.

Sarra's dirtied dress was still tucked up in her belt from climbing then running down the steep incline on the island and with all the activity and excitement it had never occurred to her to remedy the situation.

"Fern is your brother, but it is wholly unfitting in front of Sten and Mage Ichor, and all of these friends of your father's" she admonished in a whisper.

"Mistress!" Mage Ichor rose to his feet and stepped off the boat. "I am sure you speak with the best of intentions, but in my charge, acting for and working with me, Sarra is an Affine! An Affine will clothe themselves as befits the task in hand, and Affine Sarra has done just that!"

"Perhaps, Sarra, as everyone seems to have gathered to celebrate your departure with me, to Mage College, it would be wise to change, before a celebratory lunch." the Mage bowed to Sarra, who took his words to heart, and made for the house.

Sarra went to her bedroom to find a clean new set of clothes laid out over her stool next to the dresser and a pile of neatly folded clothes on top of an empty back sack on the bottom of her bed. She now had all the clothes she needed, and more, of go to Mage College. Tears welled up in her eyes and she turned to see her aunt entering the room. Her Aunt's arms reached out for her and wrapped around her.

"Would she be proud of me?" Sarra asked, tearfully.

"Oh yes! She would be fit to burst with pride." said her aunt, through her own tears. "Now get changed, and out to eat with your friends that have come to help this family.

Sarra still felt quite weak from her experience of robbing the stone of so much weight and allowed her aunt to take her arm and lead her out to lunch.

There was not enough room for everyone to be seated, but food was plentiful. Kiera, Aquila, Guyor, Trembil and Hetta kept the table replenished from the food they had prepared in the indoor kitchen.

The fishermen sat on the edge of the veranda as they had before, Brewer Fester returned in the middle of the afternoon with another barrel of ale.

"I told you that your courtyard wasn't big enough and that you needed another table and benches." the Mage's voice was jovial as it drifted over the heads of the exhausted diners. "And this is just the beginning!"

No more work was done that day. It was well into the evening when the small flotilla of fishing boats left for home, home for many being around Torroja, Hallon from further north at Santa del Ora, and two fishermen hailing from the salt-flats at the northern end of the lagoon.

The flickering lights of their lanterns dwindled in the distance as Sarra, the Mage and the four Affines sat at the table, Kiera, Guyor and Trembil having left earlier on the Mage's donkey cart.

"You can look forward to many more gatherings such as that, if Sarra chooses to return home to set up her 'Tower'." The Mage was addressing Arron, but it was a slightly drunken Sten that responded.

"Do I have to build a Tower too? There is probably nearly enough stone."

"No. No, not unless Sarra needs, or desires a view. Wherever a Mage works from is called a Tower, even if it is not." explained the Mage.

Arron gazed across at Sarra.

"She may not set up her tower here, but once we've finished building, her room will always be ready for her." Arron raised his hand to stop her objection. "I know you say that you are coming here to set up a Tower, and this will always be your home, but many things may happen to cause you to change your mind. You might fall in love while you are away at Mage College, or you might head for the bright and lighted streets of Kingsholm, we can't compete with that."

"It has been known for Affines to head there." stated the Mage. "However, we do try to discourage it. Also, Kingsholm already has a Mage who is fiercely jealous of his status in that city. Even I do not like to cross him."

Sarra decided not to argue, but just to reiterate the facts: "This is my home. My father, sister and brother live here. I have four potential Elementals here to work with, who I know and can trust, although I don't believe for one moment that my father will ever give up fishing."

"I still breed mouflons." the Mage interrupted. "Though I do not spend nearly as much time with them as I would like, or I once did. Even Mage's need a hobby!"

Sarra ignored him and went on. "This is where I created my first garden, from my mother's garden and made my own fruit orchard, surrounded by vines. This is where I shall return when my training is done."

Arron put his arm round his younger daughter. "This is your home and always will be, it will be your garden whether you tend it or not. But you don't know what the future holds, and you don't have to come home if your life takes another direction. You don't have to worry about the building works. Now that I have the stone, I can pay for the rest from my savings. I am not reliant on the Mage's promise of the College paying half, and I could always take another apprentice or two to fill it!"

Sarra thought that it was the longest speech she had ever heard her father make, with the exception of the one to the fishermen that afternoon, perhaps speech-making was habit forming!.

"I SHALL return. But for now, I am going to bed."

Sarra and Aquila rose from the table. "Me too, though we'll be able to rest more after she's gone." Aquila gave her sister a hug to take any sting out of the words.

"Well at least it will be a quieter day tomorrow." said Fern rising. "With a pleasant sail up the lagoon, and no great surprises"

"No promises!" said the Mage, almost to himself, as Fern and Sten left the courtyard.

Only Arron was left to hear the comment and to wonder what the Mage had meant and hope that he wasn't clairvoyant.

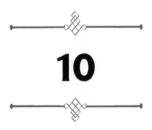

10

The morning dawned bright and clear, as did most mornings on the lagoon at this time of year. Sarra was up early to complete her chores, so everyone else arrived to find yoghurt, honey and dried fruits on the table for breakfast, the yoghurt culture set for the next day, and, if they could have seen her, a contented nanny goat grazing the field with her new friend Vessus. In the kitchen sat baskets of eggs, salad greens, and fruit, with jugs of wine and water beside them, though Sarra was confident they would find fresh water on the isle.

Everyone present was eager to be off on their trip to the Isla Grossa, and its Tower, 'Mage's Retreat', so it was not a leisurely meal. Just as they were finishing, the Mage's donkey and cart returned, with Guyor and Trembil. Guyor boiled eggs and washed salads and she and Trembil carried the food and the jugs down to stow in Swallow, for the trip.

Guyor said that she would attend to the dishes before starting on the garden and that later she would prepare them dinner from the shellfish that Trembil intended to collect.

"Dinner will be waiting for you when you get back, I think mother and father are coming to say goodbye to you too, Sarra." Guyor said.

Soon they were all aboard The Swallow. Trembil helped Arron push the boat into the shallows, then waved them off on their trip, with his sand-scoop, distracted from the job of looking for tell-tale holes in the sand, the sign of clams or razorfish being present.

With Arron at the tiller and Mage Ichor helping him to produce a strong breeze, they were soon skimming over the water, heading northwards. The island was now familiar to Arron's children and Sten and they gathered their things as they rounded the island and headed into the channel. As Arron brought Swallow alongside the quay, Fern leapt onto the stone platform with a rope, intending to tie it to the stone table.

"I thought you said that Sarra had broken the mooring ring from the quay when she lifted the boat?" the Mage was not the only one puzzled.

"She did. We took the ring home too."

Fern pulled on the shiny, new, large copper ring that was in the place of the old one. To test its strength.

"Mage-forged, I'd say."

The Mage leapt from the boat and took the mooring rope with him. He gave the ring a hefty tug before tying the rope. "Indeed!" he said. "You are sure you took it home; I suppose?"

"Absolutely." said Arron and Sten together. "And this one is new." added Fern.

"What does that mean?" asked Aquila.

"There's been a Mage on the island since your last trip." said Mage Ichor.

With a cry: "Onwards!" the Mage started up the worn path at quite a pace. He rounded the rocks and ignored the cluster of devastated houses to move straight on towards the Tower.

"Look!" cried Aquila pointing to the small cemetery they had visited before. "There are flowers on the graves." The area of crosses had been strewn with bright flowers, which were still fresh.

"Then there have definitely been people here." said the Mage, increasing his pace. The others all followed close behind. They didn't want to risk missing anything. The door of the Tower stood half open, although Sarra would have sworn that Aquila had pulled it shut behind her.

They followed Mage Ichor into the Tower and up the staircase to the second floor. The Mage had paused briefly to glance through the two open doors before moving up the stairs again. The Mage stopped at the head of the stairs, causing the other to cluster behind him on the stairway. Even from that distance they were greeted by a strong pungent smell that caught in the back of their throats. As the Mage moved forwards and they followed, the third floor came into view. Sarra gasped in dismay – all of the shelves were empty! All the specimens of plants and insects and small animals that she had not been able to identify, had now gone. She would not get the time to examine them, that she had wanted. Near the shelving, on the floor was a broken glass jar and a large squid lay amongst the glass shards, in a pool of liquid.

"What is that smell?" asked Sarra, almost choking on her words.

Preserving fluid." answered the Mage. "You may meet it again at Mage College I'm afraid. A foul liquid, but extremely useful. Didn't you say that these shelves contained specimen animals and plants?"

"Yes." confirmed Sarra. "The shelves were quite crowded with them."

They were relieved to leave the smell behind and mount the next set of stairs, still following Mage Ichor. On the table in the room on the next floor there were just two broken quills and a cracked ink vial. The other quills and vials were gone and the pile of parchment missing. The Mage hardly hesitated, but rushed on ahead, floor after floor.

On reaching the top floor, and again. pausing for their eyes to adjust to the light, the map drew everyone's attention. There was again a tiny model of Swallow sitting on the water next to the quay, but now its pale cream sail was intact and the mooring ring in place.

The Mage cried out and rushed around to the opposite side of the huge map table, drawing their attention to the model boat in the centre of The Wide Channel to The Great Sea. It was moving fast, and, before the Mage could reach it, reached the edge of the map and winked out of existence.

"DID YOU SEE THAT?" roared the Mage in frustration.

"Yes, it was a boat larger than my Swallow, with a square sail and with what looked like two canoes fixed either side of it." Arron wasn't bowed by the Mage's anger, as he knew it wasn't directed at him.

"You only use a square sail if you know the wind is blowing where you want to go, or if you can create such a wind, and the outriggers are to give more stability in large seas, or when travelling faster, so that you don't capsize." the Mage had seen such vessels before.

The Mage scratched at his chin through the growth of his beard, staring at the spot where the boat had disappeared.

"HA!" shouted the Mage, showing better humour. "They probably saw us coming!"

"I bet that put the wind up them! That is probably why someone dropped a specimen jar they were packing! We will have disrupted all their plans! Let us go and take a look around and see what else we interrupted."

As they left the tower the Mage took Sarra aside.

"Sarra, forgive me. I did believe you had powers and have felt your strength when we worked together on the rocks, but I had thought that perhaps the map was partially broken. It is not broken at all, of course, which means that no-one but it's creator should have been able to access it, let alone an untrained Mage, which you obviously are. Not even I could guarantee to be able to use it."

"That is understandable, Mage Ichor. I can understand why you would doubt that I had done it. I doubted it myself and I did not have your knowledge of how it should have worked. Or not worked, I suppose I mean."

Sarra and the Mage caught up with the others down at the edge of the group of houses. They were all single-story stone houses with tile rooves.

The first house was the one with melted walls, that they had seen before.

Someone had started to strip off tiles at one corner to gain access through the roof. Sten had climbed onto the roof and lowered himself in using the roof beams and was now shouting up through the gap.

"There's a wooden chest in the middle of the floor with a lot of folded clothes taken out. A few small pieces of jewellery at the bottom. That's all in here." he sounded disappointed.

The House Arron had gone into had been demolished at one corner.

"It looks as though someone was packing books into a basket and got called away. The shelf is half empty and the basket is almost full. They are mostly hand-written books, bound in the same leather. There's a few scrolls too." Arron seemed pleased at his discovery.

"Can you pass the basket out, Arron?" the Mage rushed to a shutter in the wall and tapped on it.

The shutter swung open, and Arron looked through.

"Don't you want the other books too?" he enquired.

"Yes, but I don't want it too heavy to carry. Put the scrolls in the basket. We'll put the other books in one of the carry nets with our lunch in."

By the time Arron had passed out the basket with books and scrolls and he and Sten had exited the houses, Aquila had suggested they stop for lunch.

Although the Mage was reluctant to stop the search, he was reassured by Arron's assertions that they would be eating next to the only deep water mooring and that beaching a boat on the eastern beach was impractical.

Sarra and Aquila spread their lunch out on the stone table at the harbour. Arron poured cups of wine and water for everyone. The sun had moved round while they were away and now brought the shade of a large orange tree, protecting them from the midday sun.

"I rather like the idea of a large tree providing shade in the courtyard." said Arron, his thoughts wandering ahead in time.

"Then we will leave planting holes in the courtyard tiles," said Sten in complete agreement. "On the southern side of the tables and Sarra can tell us what to plant there."

"No." Aquila protested. "Sarra must plant them. Everything that she plants grows successfully."

"Then we'll just leave the holes, until she returns." said Sten.

Although Mage Ichor had been reticent to leave the building exploration, for lunch, he seemed in no great hurry to get back. He relaxed with a cup of wine while the assembled company discussed the coming building works and improvements that could be made.

Sarra had been thinking about the Mage Map and the Mage who had made it.

"Do you know anything about the people who lived on this island?" Sarra asked Mage Ichor.

"I knew the Mage quite well, a long time ago." Mage Ichor replied, stroking his beard and staring out to sea. "In fact, we were at Mage College together and he was a good friend for a while."

"For a while?" Sarra prompted as the Mage had fallen silent.

"Yes, we learned together for many moons, each of us trying to outdo the other, but not real rivalry, just wanting to prove ourselves. We even talked of setting up a community together, recruiting large numbers of Elementals and building a new town to house us, a town of magic users."

Sarra thought that he sounded wistful. "So, what happened?"

Cridos wanted to discover things, new uses for plants and what properties minerals had, that we did not know about, how to combine them to make new substances, all sorts of things, most of which was useless and unnecessary and not practical at all. But you have to remember that there were lots of Mages then and they didn't all have to be practical. As long as you earned a living you could spend the rest of your time playing with things, experimenting and learning for learning's sake, or taking up hobbies or trying things that non-magical people could do. That would not do now, there aren't enough Mages or Affines to fulfil all the magical commissions as it is."

"Some of that sounds more like Wizardry or Alchemy than Magic." commented Sten.

"Yes, I suppose it was, they certainly had things in common. He was making new substances which anyone could make, if they set up a workshop and were given the right ingredients and a method, not just Affines and Elementals and Mages. It upset a lot of the Mage Tutors at the College too. Then Tradi, a lovely young Air Affine we both worked with, told me I was old-fashioned and hidebound and went off with Cridos and I never saw either of them again." Mage Ichor ended on that sad note.

Sarra was reluctant to ask any more questions, but Fern was not as reluctant.

"How was the destruction of the tower caused?"

"Cridos was a working Mage with eight Elementals to support his work. That made them a strong and wealthy community. They did not have much contact with anyone else in the Magical world, but that didn't matter, until the Mage Wars. When the Mage Wars came along, he was asked for help. No-one thought that he would do anything but offer it and respond to the call. People were depending on him for help to re-enforce the other Towers, but he refused to come. He said that he didn't believe in what the Mages stood for, and what they were fighting for, or how they acted towards others. He wouldn't work for them, or against them, he said. He said he would attack neither Mages nor Wizards, that he was neutral. He insisted that he was neutral! Mage Haytor, the chief Mage at that time, was incensed! He had just lost his daughter, Mage Elley, in an attack and was stricken with grief. *'If he's not with us, he's against us'*, was what he said, and he ordered an attack on Cridos and his community. The attack force came back saying that they'd had some success and that the community no longer existed. They brought many of their own wounded and dead back with them. Mage Haytor died soon afterwards, he led an attack on some Wizards, which I think he knew he wouldn't return from, almost a suicide mission. Soon after the Wizards mostly disappeared, and everything went quiet. So, we re-built what we could and went on much the same as before, but with a much-depleted force of Magic and Mages."

"A sad tale Mage Ichor."

"A sad tale, indeed, my friend. A sad tale to end on, as I fear it is time to collect those other books and make our way home,"

The Mage rose from his seat, picked up the basket of books and scrolls and carefully placed it in the Swallow.

Aquila packed the empty platters into one carry net and picked up the others to follow the Mage and Sarra up the rise.

The three men were only a moment behind them, and they arrived almost together at the settlement.

The Mage and Sarra peered through the shutter of the house with the books, Sarra regretting wearing a dress and not trews, the Mage wishing he were young and svelte again. Fern slipped between them and clambered through the opening. Aquila passed him a carry net, which was filled and passed back in no time at all. Fern climbed back out of the building. The Mage turned and surveyed the village.

"I wonder which house belonged to Cridos." he mused, then asked: "Where are Sten and Arron?"

As they looked about, a small wooden chest was pushed through the part dismantled roof nearby. First Sten and then Arron clambered through and off the roof.

"We thought we might as well recover this too." explained Sten.

"I think the other buildings will have to wait for another time." said Mage Ichor.

"Do you think there will be another time?" asked Sarra.

"I am sure there will. For you, at least, if not for me." the Mage replied sadly.

Sten hoisted the small chest onto his shoulder and Arron took one of the carry nets of books from Aquila, along with the two blankets they had left before. The entire group was unhappy at leaving the dwellings still unexplored, but the shadows were growing as they made their way back to the quay.

The Mage climbed aboard Swallow first, Aquila and Arron passing him the books to stow. Fern boarded, to be passed the chest by Sten. Sarra stepped on board and set about raising the sail, while Sten untied the rope and cast off, leaping board as Swallow drifted away from the quayside.

Fern held the tiller and guided Swallow out of the inlet, where they encountered a slight breeze, which Arron intensified. Part of the way home, the Mage seemed to rise from the stupor he had been in, looked ahead to where they were going, and the breeze freshened into a strong following wind.

The Swallow approached its home beach, Arron looking for space between all the boats beached there, most of them the same ones which had hauled stone just the day before.

"Not a word to anyone about where we've been or what we found!" cautioned Mage Ichor.

"Arron, you and the girls greet your guests, Fern and Sten, take the books and chest out of sight, first." the Mage organised.

As they made their way up the beach, they passed a fire with a large pot, (not their pot, Sarra noted), of octopus stew, and a rack of skewered fish, vegetables and prawns. In the courtyard, Aunt Kera presided over a pot of shellfish stew and Guyor dished out salad greens and Hetta gave out her bread rolls.

Two casks of ale that Arron did not recognise were being looked after by Brewer Festor, one having been broached some time before.

Uncle Seth had brought a huge basket of sweet pastries.

They had returned, not to dinner, but to a farewell feast.

The fishermen were far enough into the ale to be playing their instruments and singing sea-songs and even starting their sea-dances. Two old fishermen were sitting near the courtyard, telling tales of the sea, sea creatures and far-flung lands that few land-dwellers believed existed.

The six returned travellers were urged to eat and drink to catch up with those who had been there a while. Eventually Arron was prevailed upon to give a speech, praising his younger daughter, and wishing her every success at Mage College. Many people cheered and told her how much they would miss her, and her special growing touch and the fishermen presented her with a necklace, belt buckle, comb and pins made from mother of pearl and another set with coral which she knew must have been traded from the East. Her spice-seller wore a coral pin.

Sarra had been moving from one well-wisher to another, thanking them for coming to see her off, and hearing them sing her praises and wish her luck, when she came finally to her aunt. Her aunt took her by the arm and steered her towards her room.

"Sarra, you have to be fresh for the morning. I have laid your clothes out for tomorrow including your new sandals. Everything else is packed in your back sack. Do not worry about your father, the house, the animals or the garden, Guyor, Trembil and I will look after them. Now go and get some sleep, you have a long journey tomorrow!" Sarra was pleased to take her aunt's advice and slipped quietly away to her bed.

11

There had been no gull's cry to wake her, no boat scraped over the shingle, no people moved about or chatted yet and the sun was not high enough to disturb her. So, what had wakened her?

Her thoughts coalesced. It was today! Today was the day she was setting off for Mage College! That was enough to disturb anyone, even if they were asleep! This was the day on which the rest of her life began! Sarra swung her legs out of bed. Would the goat and chickens even be awake yet? No matter: if she was going to tend them for one last time, it had to be now. Sarra looked at the pile of clothes that her aunt had laid out for her, went past them to the chest at the bottom of the bed and pulled out an old pair of trews and a tunic. She did not bother with underthings but pulled them on and fastened her sandals.

She moved outside and put yoghurt, honey and fruits out for breakfast.

She fed the chickens on the way to the goat and left the egg basket by the path for the journey back. After milking the goat she picked up the well-worn milking stool, and made her way up the field to where three woven skeps sat in the rough grass, surrounded by wild flowers. She settled her stool between them and as the bees buzzed around her she told them of her fears, her plans and her dreams – or, at least, she tried to; the first was easy, but difficult to express; the second a little vague and she had no idea where to go with the third yet. So, in the end, she just told her the facts she knew:

"I'm going to Mage College; I am going in a donkey cart with Mage Ichor, today; the people in the town think I'm going to be an Affine like father, Aquila and Fern, but I'm not attracted to any element; Mage Ichor says I'm going to be a Mage, but I'm not so sure; Gaynor and Aquila will look after you all, and ask Niome if they are unsure, and the goats and the chickens and the gardens; father is taking an apprentice and going to expand the house; there are a lot of changes coming for all of us, my Queens; and I'm rambling…and I don't like change…and I wish I was staying here with you and father and the others…..and I was just making plans for alterations in the garden…..I'm going to miss you all so much and I don't know when I'll be back…..but I will be back…

Sarra wiped her cheeks on the heels of her hands to dry them, then, picking up the stool, and taking milk and eggs to the indoor kitchen, she left them for Guyor to deal with.

Back in her room she washed all traces of her crying from her face, returned her old clothes to the chest, with the old sandals and dressed in the things Aunt Kera had laid out.

She sat in front of the mirror, undid her plait and combed through her hair. She leaned forward and spoke to the image in the mirror:

"You are going to Mage College today, with Mage Ichor; you are going to learn wonderful things and become a Mage; mother would be proud of you; father and Aquila, Fern and Sten are proud of you; they are going to be your Elementals when you come back; today is the beginning of the re-forming of your life as a Mage."

Sarra parted her hair and formed two plaits which she wound round her head and secured with pins.

"This is the new you!" she told herself.

She stripped her bed of sheets and left them in a corner to be washed. Trembil would be using her room and sleeping in her bed tonight, and she would be sleeping – where?

She went out to breakfast and found her brother Fern and his friend Sten already there, eating.

"I win!" crowed Sten.

Fern explained. "He said it would be you that had put out breakfast. I said that you would be sleeping in. My bet was on Guyor or Aunt Kiera."

Sarra smiled and ignored them, helping herself to breakfast.

"Nice dress, is it new?" Sten joked. All her dresses were new, having only just moved out of tunic and trews and into adult clothes, then needing more to take with her to Mage College.

"That green suits you. It matches your eyes." Sten's compliment was sincere.

They heard the braying of two donkeys greeting each other, so were warned before Aunt Kiera, Uncle Seth, Guyer, Trembil, Crammer and Hirst walked around the corner of the house. Hirst ran to Sarra and threw her arms around Sarra's neck.

"You're going away!" she cried.

"Yes, darling, I know." replied Sarra, loosening Hirst's arms enough to breathe.

"So is Trembil, he's going away to 'prentice." sobbed the little girl.

"Yes, darling, but he'll only be here with Uncle Arron, I am sure you'll see him often."

"Will you be with Uncle Arron 's'well?" the tears ran down Hirst's face as she looked up hopefully.

"No, darling, I'll be going to Mage College with Mage Ichor." Sarra gestured to Mage Ichor, who had just put in an appearance. Hirst peered at the Mage and burst into fresh tears.

"I won't be gone that long." placated Sarra, knowing it would seem like an age to the little girl.

"We didn't really get chance to say goodbye properly last night, so we came to see you off this morning." Seth explained.

"No." said Sarra. "Where did all those people come from?"

"Well, all of your friends from the fishing community and from the town wanted to say goodbye, too. So I invited them over" replied Kiera. "But they brought ale and bread and octopus stew and lots of other things, so they fed themselves." added Kera.

Arron and Aquila appeared for breakfast. Arron grabbed Hirst under her arms and swung her high in the air.

"And how's my little Hirst?" he asked her. "And have you seen my new donkey?"" Hirst screamed and then collapsed into giggles.

"Yes, we brought him home for you, cos he came to our house. Did you know he is called Vessus?"

"No, I didn't know that, but I can guess who named him." said Arron, looking at Sarra.

Breakfast turned into quite a party. Uncle Seth gave Sarra a pair of copper combs and some pins for her hair, to mark her departure. He had also made her a long, green dyed, plaited leather belt.

Trembil took Crammer down to Arron's boat on the beach, to show him the boat that he would be working on, and to air his new-found knowledge to an appreciative audience.

Mage Ichor put down his spoon from breakfast and announced: "It is time for us to depart. I know that your relatives have come to see you go but long farewells are, on the whole, unproductive." Then to Fern, he said: "If you could bring the College's cart and donkey nearer, we will load it up."

The Mage fetched his light back bag from his room and Sarra fetched hers, her cloak folded over her arm. Aquila took Sarra's cloak from her and folded it further and put it on the front seat as a cushion. Both back bags were stowed behind the seat and Arron brought the Mage's newly acquired basket of books and stowed that on the cart too, along with a net of scrolls.

The Mage mounted the seat and took up the reigns. Sten appeared with another net of books and swung that up on top of the basket.

Sarra kissed everyone goodbye, and Arron helped her climb up and settle herself, and with a wave of her hand they were off.

As they passed through Corvanna it seemed that almost all the people she knew came to the doors of their houses and workshops to wave to her and shout a greeting. Janus was standing on the step of the moneychangers and although the money changer waved to her, Janus just turned away. For a moment Sarra felt hurt, then found that she could live without his approval, and called goodbye to Hetta and Fester. They left the little town and made their way towards the King's Highway, a few leagues further on.

When they reached the King's Highway the Mage turned the cart to the right to head northwards. They picked up speed on the smoother road surface. Sarra had never travelled on the King's Highway before, her father had brought her to it, as a child, to wave at the King as he passed. She recalled that he had ridden in a brightly painted open coach, pulled by two horses and been surrounded by soldiers on horseback. No-one had ridden a donkey! After driving through the countryside for a while they passed a collection of buildings, including an inn with people eating and drinking outside at rough wooden tables and a paddock containing horses and donkeys.

"A way station," the Mage explained. "For travellers, for refreshments and changes of horses and donkeys. Some have overnight accommodation too. They are maintained by the King's orders."

As they moved through the countryside heading north, the fields became lusher and greener, the orchards seemed to contain taller more productive trees.

The sun moved higher in the sky and Sarra took sips of water from the jug they had brought with them but looked longingly at the seats in the shade when they passed another way station.

"We shall stop at the next one, Sarra, and change the donkey too, for he grows tired and wants a drink. I am afraid I have been much occupied with my thoughts and not been a good travelling companion. Having seen where Cridos lived, and probably died, I have had much to think about."

"Not at all, Mage Ichor." said Sarra politely. "I have enjoyed the ride and the change of scene. I fear I know little of the world outside my home."

"I should be telling you so much, about Mage College; about the training and the things you will learn; about the Country itself; about the Royal Family, who you are likely to meet and about your future."

"I thought that you said that the future was unknowable and would depend on my choices?"

"That is true, my dear, but it will probably follow one of several almost pre-determined paths. If you are going home, as you insist, there will be many tempting offers you will need to resist. If you have three or possibly four Elementals in mind, you will also need to resist many, many possible Elementals who will wish to work with you. You may, indeed, be their only chance of ever being an Elemental, and not merely an Affine, as so few working Mages exist these days. I am one of only thirty-two fully trained Mages left in this country, and myself and two others are not working Mages, as such, we deal only with training. The Mage College is run mainly by administrators on loan from the King, to make up for the lack of teaching Mages, and by Myself, Mage Indigo and Mage Mandez. I have not been away from the College for this long, for many years, it has been quite a holiday! But then, we have not had a potential Mage for three years, so it was essential that you be brought safely to Mage College as soon as possible."

"Three years?" Sarra was incredulous. "I thought you had people coming to Mage College all the time!"

"Oh, we do. People come to be trained as Affines, like Aquila and Fern and Sten. Their affinity for their element is trained and increased, so that they can undertake commissions in their own area of expertise, as individuals. But they are not Elementals, and cannot undertake the tasks that an Elemental, working with a Mage, could do. It is, if you like, a weaker form of magic, a poor imitation of what real magic should be. We have not had a potential Mage to train for three years! I should have been spending my time telling you all of this and not trying to unthink my past mistakes!"

Mage Ichor guided the donkey off the highway, down a side road towards a way station.

"We will talk more in a while." he promised.

Mage Ichor turned the donkey cart over to a uniformed boy who came forward to take the reins.

"A change, refreshments and privacy." the Mage told him.

They were taken, by a small, uniformed girl, to a table in the shade. Another girl in the same uniform brought jugs of water and wine, with two beakers. She was followed by a third, similarly dressed girl carrying platters of vegetables and meat and gravy. When a uniformed boy brought them a basket of bread, he was followed by a young woman with blond, curly hair and a wide smile.

"Mage Ichor." she said, as she curtseyed. "I am returning from an assignment..."

"I thought I said PRIVACY?" shouted Mage Ichor at the boy, pointedly ignoring the young woman. The Mage turned his back on her and helped himself to bread.

Sarra shrugged at the young woman and poured wine for herself and the Mage. The Mage placed sliced meat on top of the bread and passed it to Sarra.

"We won't stop long, then we'll reach the College tonight."

Sarra took the proffered food, scooping up some steamed vegetables with her other hand and popping them in her mouth. *'Man cannot live without the fruits of the earth.'* she thought. One of her father's favourite sayings.

She ate the bread and meat, then slipped away to relieve herself, before returning to drink more wine and some water, while she waited for the Mage to finish.

The Mage led Sarra to the parked carts and helped her mount their cart. The donkey had been replaced with a sturdy and fresh-looking horse. The Mage paid the boy holding the reins and they were passed to the Mage after he had mounted the seat.

As they approached the Highway again, they saw a hay cart, held stationary by the driver to allow a group of young people to clamber on the back. The young woman who had approached the Mage was among them and looked up as they passed by. All of the young people wore travelling cloaks draped around their shoulders. There were two men left behind with the haycart crowded. The haycart moved off towards the highway, so the Mage pulled their cart over and the men ran up and climbed onto the rear end of their cart. The moment they were aboard, the Mage shook the reins and the cart moved off. They arranged their cloaks into large pads under themselves for comfort. The Mage didn't slow during the process, didn't speak to them, or show any sign that he had seen them board. They turned onto the King's Highway once more and were soon moving at a brisk trot.

For a while the only sounds were the horse's hooves drumming on the road and the murmur of the two men conversing in the back of the cart.

There came into view a side road with two figures draped in travelling cloaks.

"One thing that you may not know," the Mage began, almost conversationally. "The travelling cloak worn by a Mage or Affine, obliges travellers having room, to offer a ride, as long as they are not taken off their route."

"But how does the traveller with enough room know where they are going?" Sarra wanted to know.

The Mage smiled and leaned in secretively. "Well, they could always ask! But this close, there is only one place they are likely to be going and that is where we are going." The Mage was slowing the cart.

They reached the side road where the man and woman were waiting and came to a halt. The Mage stopped just long enough for the man to lift the woman onto the cart and scramble on himself, before they were on their way at a brisk pace.

The man crawled forwards to just behind the raised seat. "May we introduce ourselves to your companion?" the man asked.

"You may NOT!" replied Mage Ichor. Then said to Sarra: "They want to know who you are: if you are a new Affine recruit and why you are travelling with me. You will probably meet them in time, just not today, and you will NOT appraise them of your status, it could spoil your training."

"My status, Mage Ichor?" questioned Sarra.

"None of the trainee Affines are to know that you are a trainee Mage. You will adopt their status." instructed the Mage.

Sarra said nothing. She tried to listen to the conversations in the back of the cart but could hear nothing of note.

Taking sips of water to help her through the heat of the day, Sarra found her head nodding, and then sitting up suddenly with a jerk, realised that she slept through a large part of the day There was a high stone wall running alongside the highway, and looking back, had been for some time.

"What is the wall?" Sarra asked the Mage.

"Ah, I did wonder when you would ask. It is the outer wall of the

Mage College. The main complex will be coming up soon, we have made good time."

Sarra looked around and realised that the sun was dipping towards the horizon to their left. She also realised that she must have dozed for longer than she had thought. Shortly after that, they approached large gateway set back to the line of the wall. The gates stood open and there were no guards or sentries to check them. The Mage just turned into the gateway, drove under the arch and stopped. Their four fellow passengers slipped down from the cart and came to the front, beside Mage Ichor.

"Thank you, Mage Ichor."

"Thank you for your company, Mage Ichor."

"Thank you for your charity, Mage Ichor."

The young woman merely dropped a deep curtsey.

Mage Ichor said nothing but nudged the horse into motion and moved on through into the town. For a town it seemed to be, workshops and houses facing onto the street they drove though, and scores of people were going about their business, whatever that was. Their passage was noticed, watched or remarked upon by almost all the people they passed, it seemed, but the Mage acknowledged no-one and did not speak to anyone, just kept the cart moving at a steady, slow pace.

The Mage eventually stopped outside a building with two pairs of huge double doors set into its walls. Two boys came out of a side door, one took charge of the horse's head, the other took the reins from Mage Ichor and listened to his orders.

"The basket and net of books, the net of scrolls and my back bag are to be taken to my personal lodgings."

"Yes, Mage Ichor."

"The ladies back bag is to be taken to the lady Affine's lodgings, and Affine Sarra is to have her own lodging room there."

"Yes, Mage Ichor."

"Inform Mage Indigo and Mage Mendez of my return."

"Mage Indigo will be informed immediately, Mage Ichor. Mage Mendez is away at present, Mage Ichor."

"Affine Sarra and I will take refreshment in the dining hall."

"Yes, Mage Ichor."

They dismounted from the cart, and crossed the street to another large, stone building, which they entered.

Sarra had arrived at Mage College. She found that she was acutely aware of her childhood being behind her, but still had no idea as to what lay ahead.

Lightning Source UK Ltd.
Milton Keynes UK
UKHW010147030821
388208UK00008B/631/J